The Last Day of June

Ted Bun

Copyright © 2020 Edward Yeoman

All rights reserved.

ISBN: 9798644708192
Imprint: Independently published

To Grace and Adam
1st day of June 2024

Ted Bear
x

DEDICATION

This dedicated to the young lady who sat next to me to watch Al Stewart play this song, twice, some forty year apart.

Valerie

CONTENTS

France 1934 3
England 1934 9
Germany 1934 19
France 1939 25
England 1939 29
Germany 1939 33
France 1940 - 1 39
France 1940 - 2 43
France 1940 - 3 47
France 1940 - 4 53
France 1940 - 5 61
France 1940 - 6 69
France 1944 75
30,000 Feet 1944 81
Bordeaux 1944 89
France 1946 95
England 1946 101
Germany 1946 109
France 1952 117
England 1952 121
Germany 1952 133
France 1960 136

England 1960 143
Germany 1960 147
France 1967 151
England 1967 159
Germany 1967 165
France 1974 - Morning 169
France 1974 - Lunchtime 175
France 1974 – Dessert 181
France 1994 185

ACKNOWLEDGMENTS

One autumn evening in 1974, I sat on the Dining Hall floor in Elliott College at the University of Kent, Canterbury to watch a concert performance by Al Stewart.
During the show he performed most of the songs from his just released album "Past, Present and Future." Out of all the incredibly good material he performed that night two songs stuck out for the wonderful images they created in my mind's eye.
"Soho, Needless to Say" was one, the other was the inspiration for this book.

"The Last Day of June 1934"

Thank you, Al.

If I ever write a story called "Soho" you'll know what is coming

On the notorious Night of the Long Knives forces loyal to Adolph Hitler moved to eliminate opposition and challengers to Hitler's position as leader of the Nazi party. Eighty-five political figures were executed without trial. The threatening power of the irregular SA, the thuggish Brown Shirts, was curtailed. Any potential opposition had lost all senior leadership overnight. In a single swift action, Hitler had consolidated power in his hands. The date?

The Last Day of June 1934

Edward Yeoman

France 1934

The morning is humming. The heat is almost unbearable. The cicadas are deafening with their busy, scratching noise. The birds are circling overhead, high in the clear, bright blue, sky, searching for the flying insects. From where we are lying, under the shade of a small stand of olive trees, I can just see the church tower of Perinac. I squint. By looking carefully through the heat haze, I can see the clock; it's a quarter past nine.

I should be working, there are a million vines between here and the Pyrenees. I might not have to prune, trim and train them all but there is plenty of work for me and hundreds of others like me down in the vines. More than enough labour for all of us and for what we are being paid I am not sweating my balls off working in this killing heat.

The work may not be getting done but I'm not being completely idle on this searing, sunny Saturday morning. I had some company, the very pleasant company of the farmer's wife. She is my employer, my lover and, over the years since I had first walked into this small farm on my beat towards the distant mountains, we had added friendship to the mix. As I am lying looking up into the clear blue sky, I feel her reaching for my relaxed member stroking it, kissing me as it stiffens. Then she straddles me and rides me, faster as she recognises my growing urgency. Moments later it is over, for now. She slumps forward onto my chest, her head resting on my shoulder.

I relax and watch the martins chasing the insects across the sky. I realise that while life could be hard, that lying here, relaxing after making love to a good woman, life has been kind to me. A regular job, with regular meals and the affection of a woman, who is so much more than just a friend of mine.

She has fallen asleep, her naked breasts pressed against my stomach, my stomach that is still full of the breakfast she brought out to me almost two hours ago.

'Yes,' I think, 'she is so much more than a friend of mine.' I gently stroke her shoulders and she sighs and moves slightly, displacing her headscarf. Loosening it, allowing her dark tresses to escape, I lift a strand and study the colours, letting it fall, a few fine hairs at a time, watching, as the sun highlights the reds and browns in her hair.

"I really should have stopped you doing that." She re-ties her headscarf. "A good wife always keeps her hair concealed from the gaze of others."

"I have to go and prepare lunch for

Henri," she announces an hour later. "Maybe you can do a little work while I am gone. I'll be back with your lunch later. If little Louis is stiff, I will give him a little rub down too."

She is still laughing when she turns to give me a little wave as she skips through the vines towards the farmhouse. I pull my shirt back on and refastening my trousers.

Henri Menton is a lucky man, much luckier than he deserves. The youngest of four brothers, he had been the only one to come home in 1918 and had inherited the family farm. He had then been picked and groomed to be the husband of my good friend, Hélène. The offer of a generous dowry had sealed the contract between the 25-year-old veteran and the virgin of just 14 summers.

Sadly, for Henri's mother, while one of her sons had come home, it appeared his manhood would never return from Verdun. She died without grandchildren.

A few years later, when the young Louis Verdier first arrived at the farm, looking for work, he had discovered an 18-year-old, sexually awakened young wife. A young woman, who was still almost as virginal as she had been on her wedding night, and for several months after that.

I am an itinerant worker; I work the vines

and used to pick the grapes from the hills of the Pyrenees right across France to my hometown of Nantes, where the Loire runs into the sea. Now my beat runs from the Corbières Hills across the Aude and into the high vineyards above St Chinian and Faugeres. This shorter beat has allowed me to develop relationships with the landowners and spend more time with each one. Although my relationship with the other farmers are not as strong as they are with this small Perinac farm.

I stop here four times each year, coming north doing the pruning and the picking, then heading south to start each cycle. I often stay a few days on the way south, exchanging bed and board for some light work in the fields. Of course, I take some time to enjoy the company of Hélène.

When the rain falls, as it does quite often in the spring and late autumn, I wish my life had been different. That the cottage, tucked in this little valley, was home to me and Hélène. Life is what it is though and, for now, apart from a few nights, the fields of France are a home to me.

I work under the blazing June skies for an hour before the heat defeats me and I retire to the shelter of the olives again. A little later, I see Hélène returning, she is carrying a basket with bread, cheese, a little dried sausage and two stone bottles, one of water, the other full of cool wine.

Little Louis seems to be as pleased as I am to see refreshment heading our way.

Later, with hunger, thirst and carnal needs satisfied, we relax, dozing in the dappled shade of the trees. I wake as a shiver runs down my spine, something is different, I sense change. I look around, no sign of Henri, the sun is still high in the sky, the vines still, unmoving far into the hazy distance. Something big is going to rock the world on its axis. I can't tell what or when, I am about to start exploring the thought, Hélène's hand reaches for me and … 'Ah, but today' little Louis interrupts my gloomy thoughts. 'Lying here is a good place to be!' My hand reaches for her and I pull her closer.

She responds and locks me in a crushing embrace, holding me tight to her, tight inside her. I can't go anywhere, not that I want to. It is as if she has felt the same change in the air. We make love furiously at first, then more gently, caring for each other but as we slip in and out of embrace, we have changed.

She still feels and looks unchanged, like some old and familiar place, that looks the same but has changed in some minor detail. Something in me is different I realise. I want more for us, I want there to be an us. I look in her eyes and I see her reflecting all of my dreams in her face. A change has occurred and our love can never be like before…

On the last day of June 1934

England 1934

"Come on Charles, it will be fun. Heather will be there!" Why Giles is so desperate for me to accompany him to this damn party? I have no idea. I have never understood why Giles, or should I say Viscount Giles de Urville, a direct descendant from one of William's Norman Knights, demands the company of me, the son of an armament manufacturer. All right, my father is as rich as Croesus and had paid for me to go through Harrow and Kings. The de Urville family, however, could buy him out from the small change down the back of a few of the many sofas that littered de Urville House. Giles used to have a bit of a crush on me, but I had turned down all his advances. I had flaunted Mary, Cristobel and Anna in front of him. It wasn't that either.

I gave up arguing. I always did when Giles had a plan. Besides, Heather was a bit of a looker and we had sort of hit it off at the Spring Ball. We had taken tea together after that and that had gone well too. How Giles had discovered she was going to be at this party, I have no idea, but he has never lied to me.

A thunderstorm is looking increasingly likely as afternoon slides past. So, I help Giles to raise the hood on his highly polished, black Alvis Drophead. The car is his pride and joy.

It was a good thing that we did, the storm arrives when we are just out of Cambridge. The rain reduces visibility, Giles eases back on the throttle, we have plenty of time. Even with the thick clouds, it isn't dark yet. Then, on a narrow country lane, a bottle-green Bentley overtakes us, going at high speed even in the driving rain.

Giles, never one to turn down a challenge, takes off in pursuit, driving the Alvis as hard as he can. I cling on to the edge of my seat in fear of my life. Then ahead of us, I watch in horror as the Bentley slips and skids round a corner, almost out of control, then pulls straight again. Giles hits the brakes, hard, too hard, the back wheels lock. The Alvis slithers towards the hedge that lines the sides of the road. 'We are going to die,' my mind screams then, an open gate. We slide to a stop in an open field. The cows, at least I hope it is cows I can smell, must be in the milking parlour.

We sit in silence and smoke a cigarette each before turning the car around and continuing our journey.

Giles' driving, I note, is a little more circumspect. The road surfaces have remained greasy, with water running off the fields. This, despite the sun having broken through the retreating storm clouds. We arrive at the gatehouse of Denham Hall, where a gatekeeper is on duty. We show the servant our invitations. I sit back, composing myself, as Giles crunches the Alvis back into gear and heads up the drive to the door.

As we pull up to the portico, we are both surprised to see the driver of the Bentley and his passenger, still dressed for the road, standing by the big green car.

"There you are! Did you get caught behind those bloody cows too?" Mays, Johnnie Mays greets us. Where had he got a car like that?

"Yes, we had an encounter with cows, I think my car needs a clean after it too." Giles quickly covers up the real reason for our delayed arrival. "That is a rather swish machine you have there!"

"A present from my Grandfather, a reward for completing my studies." Like me, Mays is 'trade', an extra generation of wealth but still trade. The Mays' family had made a lot of money in the tea market, although there was also talk of a significant contribution from the poppy trade.

"Did you get a first or something? That is a lot of car!" I start to think that Giles is jealous. I, on the other hand, dream of a car of any sort.

"No, just the usual 'Gentleman's

degree', what else!" Mays laughs. "No, I think the old boy was just glad to see me forced out of academia. He thinks I'll contribute to the family wealth, rather than just spending it now!"

"Ah, I think my family have given up on me in that respect. Shall we join the throng?" Giles holds his arms wide to shepherd us all into the house.

We change out of our travelling clothes and go through to join the other 'bright young things' as the press refers to people like us. The party is starting to come to life as new people arrive and more of the punch is consumed. I spot Heather across the room; she is talking in a very animated manner with some chap. Time for me to take control or risk losing this game before the first ball is even bowled.

I collect a couple of cocktails from a passing tray and work my way across the crowded room.

"I brought you a drink." I hold out the glass to Heather. She smiles brightly and takes the martini from my hand. "Thank you, Charles. Shall we take them out onto the terrace?" With that, she links her arm through mine and leads me through the open French windows and out into the warm night air.

I watch her over the rim of my glass as I

sip my drink, she looks happy to see me, radiant even.

"Thank you for coming to my rescue. Rupert is about as sensitive as a brick. Just because he is my brother's friend ..." Then she flashes me another scintillating smile. "Enough about him, how have you been and why haven't you come to visit me sooner?"

Visit? The word starts the tumblers in my mind falling into place. I hardly knew our host, William, Lord Denham. I had participated in a few seminars he had run as part of his post-doctoral studies. Hardly enough to get me an invitation to one of his house parties. Nor was my reputation as a raconteur and wit for that matter. Giles, of course, knew his Lordship better, still, that didn't explain my personal invitation. It didn't explain how Giles knew Heather would be at the party either.

Now it all fits together, the invitation, the ease with which she navigates the house and the word "visit." Heather is part of the Denham dynasty. I need to dig deeper, but not too deep, obviously.

"You haven't been forthcoming with your address, I presumed there was a reason or I would have certainly paid you a visit sooner. I enjoyed our afternoon together."

"But you know now?"

"I think I do and I hope you'll want me to visit again after tonight."

"I think I might like that, Charles. Come let's walk."

An hour later, we are standing on the bridge that crosses the stream feeding the lake. From there we can see the lights of the party as they shine out over the fields. The bright moonlight lets us to see the twisting path that leads to a little folly, which stands by the water's edge, where some lovers were pretending that they were alone and unwatched. A little further along the side of the lake, the reflected light revealed occasional splashes. Some brave souls were cooling off, with a swim in the moonlit waters. As we watch the furtive couples in their not-so-secret assignations, the soft, moonlit, sky explodes in a myriad, sparkling, coloured lights.

"Fireworks! I love fireworks!" Heather bounced up and down with eager anticipation as the wave of explosions subsides. The occupants of the ballroom were pouring out on to the terrace and into the gardens. The couples around the folly were standing, looking up at the sky. Even the naked bathers, illuminated by the falling lights stand, awkwardly, awed by the spectacle of the Roman Candles shooting coloured flares high into the air over the lake. The next wave of light ripples around the gardens, the lovers and dancers stand enthralled to watch maybe twenty or thirty Catherine Wheels flare into spinning blurs of colour, one here, one there, one over yonder, all around the gardens. Then as the last one slowed, a final fusillade of rockets streak skyward to explode in an ultimate cacophony of bangs and cascading coloured lights.

In the silence that follows the last explosion, after the gasps died away, applause echoes around the gardens. In the ballroom, the band launch into a spirited Charleston and couples hurry back indoors.

Heather and I dance a few times, a foxtrot and a jive, before I get dragged into one of those earnest debates. Heather is asked to dance with another of her brother's friends and disappears. For the next hour, we argue realities, everyone digging their heels on their personal point of view. There is even disagreement over whether we are truly living in a world that's finished with war. I was part of a minority that thought that the impotence of the League of Nations, unable to quell the growing crisis in Abyssinia, where Italy is flexing its muscles, threatening another member state, seems to bode ill for a future world without war.

Giles is very disappointed to discover that the notorious homosexual Guy Burgess hadn't turned up, Giles had rather hoped he might. Burgess had been invited but had left on a trip to Russia earlier in the month. In a sulk, Giles announces that he and I have to take our leave. I find Heather and say farewell and arrange to have lunch with her the following week.

'If I had a car of my own!' I'm not usually jealous but tonight the green-eyed monster rages in my soul.

On the way back to Cambridge, I become aware that Giles has had a little too much to drink. He is not driving with his normal fluid skill. As we are passing through Cherry Hinton, something distracts him from the road. The Alvis hits the curb, there is a nasty crunch from the front suspension and the car cants to the left. Unable to continue, we decide we'll have to hoof it. Leaving our heavy coats in the car, we set off towards our digs on Shanks's pony.

The night is still warm, even after the earlier storm and a gentle zephyr, a lost wind of summer, blows as we walk into the silent streets. Walking up towards Mill Road we walk past the tramps who sleep in the alleyways by the railway lines. Across Parker's Piece and past the University Arms, where the rich visitors to the city will be tucked up in silk sheets. There is hardly a light showing and silence reigns.

Back at my digs, I am troubled by something someone had said at the party. "Trouble is coming to many corners of the world and Europe lies sleeping." The discussion had gone on, getting heated. Maybe I should have supported him more strongly, with my worries about Abyssinia. However, he had gone all melodramatic before I could intervene and in a poetic flourish, he had announced, "You think the Goddess of War is dead and buried. She may be buried but in the quiet of the night you feel her heartbeats through the floor."

I put my hand to the parquet in my room, I wasn't sure he wasn't right…

On the last day of June 1934

Edward Yeoman

Germany 1934

I wake up in a cold sweat, despite the heat of the night. The sky, through my open bedroom window, was just starting to lighten. Panicked, I reach for my diary, it's 30th, thank God!

I had dreamt that, on the night of July 1st, Ernst Rohm died. The leader of the SA, the part of The Party my youth organisation was affiliated to, had been shot. Executed, for plotting against the leadership of the Reich. Although some voices rang out, in my dream, those and all the other opposition were silenced swiftly. Even far from Munich, in the rolling Bavarian hills of southern Germany, in the northern coastal towns of Cuxhaven and Emden, from Duisburg in the west to Königsberg in Eastern Prussia, Hitler's faction of The National Socialist Party had taken control of the levers of power. The Nazis were on the march and mobs swept through the cities. Carrying swastika banners, they had smashed Jewish and communist businesses. They burned books while they sang and danced around the flames. All the while, the blood of their beaten victims was flowing red in the gutters.

The Nazis had grown strong, like lions, as their opponents had become weak, like lambs. The individual citizens had been carried along by the lies and propaganda of The Party. Their insidious suggestions the enemy within used to create hatred, fuelled the massive joining of wills against former friends and neighbours.

Oh, it was planned. Oh, it was going to be brutal and bloody. Oh, it was cynically executed.

It was such a vivid dream, a nightmare I couldn't wake from. I had seen the mobs marching, I had heard the windows being broken. I had felt the screams of those brutally beaten, crippled, maimed and killed, until they echoed away, like a roar, fading in the distance. A figure, a statue, appeared, in the moonlight, gaunt, ragged, starved, a Jew; carved out of steel. It was singing,

"All the oppressed, so low and so poor
You don't know you're wrong, very wrong
You can wound me, you're wrong and I will live on
Longer than your law."

After that horrific dream, I did not want to join my friends as they went to the Youth Camp. Helga will understand why her Emil hadn't come to Grunwald this weekend when I explained. Well, she will if she is the young woman, I hope she is.

I have taken myself for a walk, alone, away from the questioning and prying. Why was I not with the others at camp? Why am I not doing my duty to the Reich? Am I a communist sympathiser?

I can't tell them I was scared by a dream. A dream I can't understand. A dream about nothing that has happened.

If I did, I would be locked up in one of the new psychiatric hospitals they put the weak-minded in. So instead I walk alone, into the countryside to think, to try to clear my mind. Eventually, my wandering leads me back to the river. I find the quiet place where I used to sit while fishing. It is very quiet here now, the other boys are all off with various organisations training, being taught drill. Today, I am the only one left, so I sit silently by the banks of the Rhine. Dipping my feet in the cold water, I watch it stream and eddy around my ankles. It reminds me of the events in my dream, swirling and circling in the stream of time.

Slowly, I find peace and acceptance of the things I saw in the night. I know I'm a dreamer and that not all dreams come true. I know I'm out of line, I have doubts about the future, I should be like my classmates, like the other members of the Hitler Youth. These doubts put me at odds with my peers, my parents, with the people I see everywhere which scares me even more.

It is late as I wander back into the town. It is a warm summer evening. The shop workers and delivery boys are being joined by members of the various organisations that we youngsters are required to join, out on evening passes. As I walk on, couples pass by me, they're looking so good in their smart uniforms. I find my group in a coffee shop not far from the Town Hall.

"Either I ate something, or maybe I drank too much last night," I explain away my absence. "I still had my head down the closet at lunchtime!" My parents are at a Party meeting in Heidelberg for the weekend, so nobody can gainsay me.

"How much beer is too much beer for Emil to handle?"

"Two litres?"

"No, one!"

"Maybe he had a sniff of the bar maid's apron!"

"Or was it the barman you were sniffing?" The teasing went on for a short while before I divert them onto the activities at the camp this weekend. All too soon, it is getting late, the passes will expire, they must be back in camp so the party breaks up. I watch as the established couples, their arms round each other, giggle and laugh as they head for the woods. Their thoughts focussed on each other and what they were going to do together before they reach the segregated accommodation.

'They don't care who Ernst Rohm was … is', I thought, so vivid had my dream been I struggled to grasp the reality that he is still alive. My mind remains in turmoil. My thoughts and conversation have been all over the place this evening. So much so, that even though I had promised to catch up with them tomorrow morning, my friends had scoffed at the idea. They didn't believe me, and there was no reason they should...

On the last day of June 1934

Edward Yeoman

France 1939

Friday 30th June 1939

Lens

My Dearest Hélène

I am so relieved to hear that Henri has been called up and I can now write to you more openly. How is our daughter? Does she look as beautiful as you? Is she looking forward to school? Does Henri still think she is his?

We have been moved forward to an airfield just behind the border, close to the town of Lens. The aircraft arrive on Monday, we will be working hard getting everything ready all weekend. Then the patrolling will start, our aircraft are tasked with supporting the infantry between Lille and Maubeuge. Hopefully, a squadron of Bréguet bombers will make the boches think twice before attacking.

Sadly, it looks highly unlikely that I will be able to help with the vines this summer. Even if the Germans surrender tomorrow, the army will take so long to organise sending us home, we won't be home by Christmas in this war either!

Write to me soon, give our little girl a big hug from me.

Love, Louis

The news of Henri going off to Toulouse, after being called up to his Infantry Division, was in the last letter I received from Hélène. I had been lucky, the man from *l'Armée de L'Air* was looking for strong men to manhandle bombs the day I arrived at the Recruiting Office in Béziers. I had avoided having to sit in a trench, armed with a rifle, while the enemy soldiers and tanks came straight at me.

I sealed the envelope and handed it to the orderly, the mail wagon was due to leave within the hour. I had been less than truthful with the news, we all had to be to avoid the censors and the discipline we would suffer if we told the full story.

I might not be the sharpest knife in the drawer, I might not have read works of philosophy, I might not be able to do the trigonometry required to fire the big guns, but I have eyes and ears. I can interpret what I see and hear, I can add one plus one and I know that the answer is not a dozen.

Yes, we are on a flat field and have cleared the sharp stones from a strip of grass. The stones now ring an area with a sign declaring it as the 'Bomb Store'. Tomorrow, I and the rest of the armourers start digging inside the ring, piling the earth against the outside walls. Hopefully, this will stop one of our bombs blowing us all to kingdom come.

On the other side of the field, another squad are doing the same to create a fuel dump.

A third team are digging latrines, pitching tents and setting up kitchens between the two storage areas. As some wag joked, we will be living with dumps on three sides of us!

When the planes arrive on Monday, we know they won't be the modern, fast Bréguet models, although they are due soon. We will be receiving old clunkers for the aircrew to train on. Not that I care, my job is to help load the bombs into the racks, then take them out again if an aircraft returns with them unused. Brutal, heavy and potentially dangerous work, miserable, cold work in the depths of winter but, and it is a huge but, nobody was going to be shooting at me or trying to stab me with a bayonet.

I try not to dwell on these things. I prefer to remember the summers of recent past. The sun and warmth of the Languedoc, the friendly people, my days with Hélène, the bottle of Crémant and happy smile that Henri had welcomed me with when I arrived in the Spring of `35. He was celebrating the birth of his daughter, "a miracle, after all these years to be blessed with a child."

His joy, cutting me to the core; until Hélène handed me the baby, whispering, "Her eyes are the colour of her father's."

As I gazed into those grey eyes, I was filled with a realisation that the most important thing in my life must have occurred the previous summer. Was that the change we had both felt that afternoon?

I hope desperately that it was, and not what lies ahead.

England 1939

I ease the stick of the Miles Magister forward, gaining speed as we rush towards the Hawker Hind that is towing our target for this final exercise.

My head was still thumping from my day-old hangover. We had celebrated the creation of the Woman's Auxiliary Air Force with a party in College Hall Mess at Cranwell. I wasn't due to fly the next day and I had overdone it a bit. Well, it was the first celebratory party we had held since passing basic. There had only been a couple of wakes too, we had the reputation of being a lucky group.

I follow the other two aircraft in a left echelon, I would be the last to fire on the drogue before peeling away right following the other members of the flight. Provided I didn't cock up … 'What the!" I push the stick forward harder and slide underneath Red 2. Gerald had just broken the cardinal rule, he had turned across the echelon, trying to track the target.

I phone Heather from the mess, "Spitfires!" I could hardly contain myself. I had the opportunity to fly the latest RAF fighter. Gerald had been thoroughly debriefed and was booked onto the bomber conversion course. On the other hand, we were both alive. The

Mess wasn't having another blow-out to mark two blazing pyres in the Lincolnshire countryside.

After Cambridge, I had taken up a chance to learn to fly when one of the chaps who had signed up for flying lessons had a polo accident. The place on the course with the University Air Squadron was booked and paid for; no refunds were available. I had nothing else to do that week, so "What the hell! Yes, I'll do it!" And I went for it. Now, four years later, Flying Officer Charles Thornton was going to fly a Spitfire!

Even Lord William was pleased with my success. "Make Captain or whatever you flyboys call it, and I will let you marry my sister!" He had announced when my commission was gazetteered.

Now, I was one step from Flight Lieutenant, as we "flyboys" call the rank the Pongo's refer to as 'Captain'. Assigned to fly the newest weapon of war in the arsenal of the British Empire. My wife, Heather, we hadn't waited and William hadn't cut us, was inordinately pleased for me. Her delight was complete when I told her I had a week's leave. A week together, I could hear her mentally planning the trip to Cornwall we had promised each other, while we were sitting in front of the blazing Christmas fire.

Back in the Mess bar, the other members of my course were bantering with an Australian officer. He was telling tales of what he had seen and experienced flying for the International Brigade in the skies of Spain.

"What were you doing in Spain? The Australians aren't involved there are they?"

"No, I was there as a private individual, but having witnessed the fascists in action, I signed on for another ten years in the Air Force as soon as I got to London."

"You were in combat?"

"Combat? Well, I got shot out of the sky twice. First time I limped back to base, not having so much as having fired my guns. The second time I landed on the beach near Barcelona in flames."

"Did you shoot any of those Messerschmitt's down?"

"Nah, mate. They were the ones doing the shooting down. They would swarm all over us and the old crates the Russians had supplied didn't stand a chance in a dog-fight."

"Dog-fights? I thought they were impossible at speed?"

"I hope you never have to find out, son."

The Australian Airforce Officer picked up his uniform jacket and left the bar. It was then I spotted the three broad stripes on his epaulettes. A Wing Commander.

I finished my pint and slipped off, leaving the rest to celebrate their postings. I had had the joy knocked out of my evening.

The last day of June 1939 and the Goddess of War was stalking across Europe.

Germany 1939

I was home on leave, a hero of the Slovac War. Not that I'd actually heard a shot fired in anger. I had marched and ridden in trucks behind a line of Panzers toward Pilsen, our orders to secure the Skoda factory. The factory had been taken intact and the Storm Troops had hurried on towards Prague.

There was a brief flurry of excitement, in mid-March, when we were called on to parade, in the cold, alongside the road as the Führer drove past. He didn't stop, his cavalcade just continued past, speeding him on his way to Prague Castle. From where he announced the new Protectorate status for the conquered lands.

We were withdrawn from Pilsen a few weeks later. Most of the Panzers rode back on transporters, we marched. Jealous of the tank crews riding into the battle in their armoured chargers? Of course, we were!

Training, training and exercises, followed by more exercises. We crossed rivers. We transited across bogs. We traversed minefields and raced across heathlands. God help anyone who opposed us.

Then one Thursday, I could tell it was Thursday, it was Weiss kohl day in the canteen. My favourite meal of the week and I missed it.

I was summoned to Group Head Quarters. It wasn't bad news, just a single Gefreiter, with a signed order and a car. I gave my boots a quick clean and brushed most of the mud off my battle dress. Then we were off to Paderborn.

"Do you speak French, Private?" The Hauptmann demanded as I stood at attention in front of his desk.

"Yes, Sir!" I snapped back.

"In French, Brunnig, answer in French!"

"Oui, mon Capitaine."

"Good, the files are correct. Report to this office on Monday. Special training." And he gestured that I was dismissed.

I was not allowed to tell anyone that I was doing a French Translators' course. I had been promoted to Gefreiter and assigned to a support role for a section of Panzers. I was too valuable to risk in the front line but not valuable enough for a job in Headquarters.

*****

Orders have been coming in over the

past few days. A lot of Units appear to be being supplied and re-equipped to 'battle-ready' standards and then slipping away eastward. Was there more trouble fomenting in Bohemia and Moravia? Was the Führer going to open a passageway to our people trapped in Danzig as Herr Goebbels had promised?

Strange rumours circulated the camp for the past few days proved incorrect. The scuttlebutt was that we were to deploy to the western border of the Fatherland. They were wrong, in the best possible way. We were to be stood down for a week of home leave.

That is how I come to be here, lazing by the river. Helga was running her fingers through the fair hair on my chest. In a few hours, I will have to dress in my uniform and escort my wife back to my parent's house. I will say farewell to our two children and return to barracks.

Meanwhile, I have recovered enough to have another go at providing a third, young Brunnig for the glory of the Fatherland. I take her hand from my chest and roll her onto her back. I pause for a second admiring her small soft breasts, before I roll over covering them with my body as she guides me inside her.

I can hear movement in the bushes as we share a cigarette. I put my finger to my lips, urging Helga to remain still and stand up. "Stay still, if you attempt to run; I will catch you and beat you!"

I quickly pull up my trousers and push my arms into my jacket and, turning, push back the bushes. I recognise the two youngsters, crouching behind the shrubbery.

"Herr Gefreiter Brunnig!" One of them had some bottle.

"Max? and Heinrich?" I had recognised them, a couple of fifteen-year-olds from further down the street from my parents.

"Ja! Herr Gefreiter!" Max snapped back coming to attention.

"Who is your unit Komandant?"

"Oberst Schmidt, Mein Herr."

"Tell Herr Oberst Schmidt that I complimented you on your stalking skills. What did you learn from exercising these skills?"

"We saw you with Frau…" A sharp elbow in the gut from Max shut Heinrich up.

"We learnt, from a skilled Gefreiter, how to create a new generation of the master race to defend the Fatherland from its enemies."

"A good and proper answer, Max. This was your private lesson. If I find out you have told anyone else about your private lesson. You will have betrayed the trust that I and Frau Brunnig have placed in you. I will report your lack of moral fibre to Oberst Schmidt and have it appended to your record. Now go and allow my wife to dress in private." They both ran, as fast as they could.

"That was very clever, Emil. They won't be bragging, not with that threat hanging over them!" Helga having finished adjusting her underwear, bends to pick up her blouse.

"No," I gently slap her rounded buttocks, "but on the other hand they won't forget the lesson they learnt from 'a skilled Gefreiter' and his sexy wife on the last day of June 1939!"

Edward Yeoman

France 1940 - 1

"Merde!" The flak had damaged the bomb release mechanism as well as the undercarriage. There was a two-hundred and fifty-kilogramme bomb hanging in the bomb bay. The pilot had at least got his damaged plane back to the airfield, unlike six of his colleagues. The Squadron had taken a beating as it tried to stem the flow of Boche tanks and guns charging through Belgium and into France,

"What is it like under there?" My Sargent shouts above the roar of another of our remaining Bréguet bombers, as it returns to be re-armed.

"The good news is there is a primed bomb, a big bugger hanging from a single clamp," I shout back.

"That's the good news?"

"Yes Sargent, the bad news is that the clamp is bent to buggery!"

"Is it stable enough to wait while we get the wing lifted, Verdier?"

I don't know if he ever heard my reply, cannon shells thudded into airfield as at least two Me110s strafed the place. I heard guys running for cover screaming. Then something hit my head, I passed out.

When my consciousness returned, it was quiet, almost silent apart from, apart from the creaking of metal. The bomb tore loose and fell, landing on my left hand. Crushing it. I screamed in pain and passed out again.

I came around again, in agony. The pain was unbearable. Then I hear another plane approaching. A single-engine fighter, I might get lucky, a round from its cannon ending my life. It didn't, the engine died. There was the thump of a plane landing. Followed by the noise of churning grass and tearing of metal.

A shout, a foreign language, friend or foe? Another shout, "Bonjour!" The accent is awful; he must be English.

I move slightly to try to see, something. My scream must have alerted him to my presence.

A few pain-racked minutes later, a face appears under the fuselage. He looks around assessing the situation. He goes to touch the bomb.

"*Non!*" I shout, he pauses and looks at me. "BOOM!" It is all I can think of that might explain the situation.

"Ah!" It appears he understands the message. "*Votre amis?*"

My friends? Where were they? Dead? Hiding? Runaway? Or retreating?

Before I can reply, we are interrupted by the noise of heavy lorries arriving. More shouting, I am about to call out, when the look on the Englishman's face tells me they are Germans. Lots of Germans have just arrived. How long can we stay hidden? How long before the pain causes me to cry out?

Edward Yeoman

France 1940 - 2

I ease the stick forward, picking up speed as I lead the flight of Spitfires into action against the formation of Stuka dive bombers we had been ordered to engage.

"Red Leader!" There is panic in the voice crackling in my ear. "Red Three; Jerries in our…" I never learnt where young Simms had seen the Messerschmitts. A burst of static ended the transmission as I felt the impact of cannon shells on the rear fuselage of my plane.

I haul the stick back, causing my Spitfire to climb and lose speed. I pray that Red Two is far enough away to avoid flying straight into me. He is, this manoeuvre was not in our textbook, but I had seen German pilots use it against our attacks. As Red Two shoots past me with two Me109s on his tail, I push the stick forward and line up on the rearmost of the two Jerry planes. I send a two-second burst from my machine guns in his direction. I see bits fall from his wings; he spirals away. I look round for his partner; I have lost him! Then my aircraft shudders as a bust of shells rip across my left wing. He has found me.

"Keep steady, Red Leader!"

'What?' Suddenly another Spitfire

appears, filling my vision. 'Head on! I'm going to die!' The propeller wash almost tears the stick from my hands, but I don't die.

"Score one for Red Section!" I look around and can see a trail of smoke heading for the French countryside below. "Are you OK, Leader?"

I notice that the controls are heavy and the engine oil temperature gauge is nudging into the red. "I think I'll have to put her down somewhere. Head home and let them know what has happened. Red Leader out."

I look around carefully, the skies are empty. I had noticed this happening before; a full sky emptying in a matter of seconds. I look around again, I am well aware they can refill just as easily. I feather the propeller, allowing the engine to idle while I glide towards the ground, searching for somewhere to land.

'There it is! An airfield.' I glide over the airfield to attract the attention of the ground crew. A French Air Force base, I can see two, damaged twin-engine planes, however, the grass strip looks unmarked. Turning into the wind, I engage the engine, lower the undercarriage and bounce to a stop.

No sign of any ground crew, no sign of movement, except the smoke rising from the engine cowling of my Spit'. Things look rather warm under the bonnet. I realise the danger and decide that it might be better to be somewhere else. I unclip the safety harness, slide back the canopy and climb stiffly out of the office.

One look at the damage and I realise that I am very lucky to be down in one piece. The kite will need a lot of patching if it is ever going to fly again, I can see daylight right through the fuselage, in several places. There is still no sign of any ground crew though.

"Anybody here! Hello!" I shout. Then, remembering that I have landed in France, or maybe Belgium. I hope it is France, the Germans took Brussels days ago. I shout again in French, "Bonjour!"

Seconds later I hear a sound, a scream of pain. There is still no movement. I notice that there are no vehicles around either. I follow my ears towards the scream, under one of the damaged bombers. There are several bodies sprawled under the wing, I feel vomit rising in my throat when I hear another agonised whimper.

Wriggling past the corpses I work my way under the wreck. I find a man with his arm pinned under a bomb. I move to see whether I can free him, when he shouts, "No!" and makes a noise that could well be French for "Boom."

I am trying to make a new plan when I hear trucks arriving. Could it be my companion's compatriots returning?

I slither out backwards to take a look. The trucks all bear black crosses. Germans, lots of Germans. I look back to the French man, his pain is etched across his face.

France 1940 - 3

We have been advancing fast for days, the tanks have been in action almost daily since we crossed into the low countries eight days ago. This is Blitzkrieg, Lightning War. We keep moving, moving forward, crushing anything that stands in our path. We have been moving so fast that the logistics have been struggling to keep up. Fuel is the critical component, fuel for the tanks. A charging Panzer is an awesome thing, an immobile tank is a pillbox and we destroy pillboxes all day long. Fuel is my job.

"Feldwebel Brunnig!" Bloody junior officers, they know nothing, but love to lord it over us.

"Leutnant!"

"The map shows an airfield about ten kilometres south of us. Take a fuel bowser and two trucks, recover any fuel you can."

"Sir!" At least it will be just me and my squad. A bit of peace and quiet. Don't get me wrong the combat wasn't fun but neither is the 'Bull' the officer class expect. I'm glad to get away for a bit of independent action.

It takes almost an hour to find the airfield, having to hide from low-flying aircraft several times. I sent a small detachment of men to the perimeter wire to observe the state of the defences. They were back very quickly; it appears that the aerodrome is deserted. I get a machine gun mounted on each of the trucks and we crash the gate. Blitzkrieg! Everyone hit the ground running as we race toward the tented encampment. No reaction, no noise, no gunfire. The French have abandoned the place. Two of their irritating, low-level attack planes lie damaged on the grass. I was surprised to see a Spitfire sitting on the runway. Then I saw the damage, this one would no longer threaten our dive bombers.

I order the squad to search the area, find the fuel dump and anything else useful. The fuel dump and the camp kitchen were found very quickly along with the bomb dump. The extra rations were being enthusiastically piled onto one of the trucks. He might have been a Frenchman but Napoleon was right, an army, this army, marches on its stomach. It wasn't just the fuel supplies that we had been outrunning.

The other truck and the fuel bowser were at the fuel dump. It was well provisioned. We would need a second trip to secure it all. Then I got the report.

A British pilot had crawled out from under one of the wrecked French planes. His hands held high in the air. My English is not as good as my French, but I am the Regimental

Linguist, that is why I have this safe, well almost safe, role in this war. Time to find out what is going on.

"Charles Thornton, Flight Lieutenant, 612 Squadron RAF." The usual Geneva rubbish we are told to recite if taken prisoner.

"And Flight Lieutenant?"

"There is a Frenchman, trapped under that plane, a bomb has fallen on him."

"And"

"I think it is primed."

"Scheisse!" This was news I could do without. We have a vast supply of fuel here and an unexploded bomb metres way from a huge pile of explosives, enough to blow a big hole between here and kingdom come. I am not a weapon specialist, nor are any of the squad. "Take me to him!" I order the pilot.

Under the wing I can see the problem, the bomb is not stable. It could easily move, and if it went off. "Ka-Boom!"

We have a problem. I want this fuel dump emptied. I have no particular wish to take prisoners. I need this bomb made safe. The only man who might know how to do this is French, trapped underneath the bomb and in great pain.

To add to the problem, it appears that I am the only person here who can speak to the Frenchman, at least to a reasonable standard. The Englander might be able to ask him about the size of his aunt's garden but that would be the limit.

I get the trucks and the fuel bowser to move out and wait for me about a kilometre up the road, in a patch of woodland. I send the unit First-Aider in search of some supplies from the French medical tent. He comes back with some bandages and morphine. I get him to give the Frenchie a mild dose, take the edge off his pain but keep him awake. He leaves the rest of the syringe of pain killer with me, in case. In case of what we don't discuss. Meanwhile, I get a couple of 'grunts' with guns to guard the plane.

Between the two of us, aided by the morphia, the pilot and I, guided by the doped-up Frenchman, roll the bomb off his arm. I fashion a rough sling to brace the damaged arm against his body and I start to listen to instructions on how to disarm the bomb.

Tools, we need tools. The Frenchman knows where we can find them. The Englishman and I help him out from under the broken hulk of the plane. We are helping him towards the armourers' tented workshop when

I hear them. The sirens of diving Stukas.

We scatter for cover, as the wrecked Spitfire erupts into flames. Followed by first one, then the second of the French bombers. The bomb we had just moved goes off. Whether it was that or a bit of stray ordinance from the Luftwaffe, but the bomb store goes up. Seconds later, the booms and crackles of the exploding munition are drowned out by an almighty WOOF! as the fuel dump goes up.

'God in heaven, let these idiots crash in front of one of our tanks!' Anger, burning anger fuelled by visions of a stalled Panzer being shelled to oblivion. I rose to my feet as the sound of the dive bombers receded and shook my fist in fury. One of the rear gunners loosed a burst towards me. The bullets falling harmlessly around me, the range was too great.

The damage was done. The fuel had been destroyed. The two guards were dead. The prisoners, well, 'fuck the prisoners, I'm out of here!' I decide and hoof it up the road to the waiting trucks. At least they were safe.

Edward Yeoman

France 1940 - 4

That wailing scream will haunt me forever. Next time I am that close to a Stuka, I want to be emptying the guns of my Spitfire into it. The Jerry has dived for cover, very sensibly. I grab Frenchy's good arm and drag him after me as I head for the nearby woods. We don't get that far when we fall into a ditch. Frenchy screams in pain, not that it matters as the bomb and fuel dumps explode at the same time. We could have been conducting a full orchestra and nobody would have heard a thing.

Eventually, the ground stopped shuddering and heaving. There was a final clattering of a machine gun and it went silent. We sat silent, waiting. I have no idea what Frenchy was waiting for. I was waiting for my legs to stop shaking. In the distance, I heard truck engines starting then ... silence.

I shared a smoke with the Frenchman and redid the strapping holding his crushed arm to his chest. I tried very hard to make sure he understood that he must see a doctor as soon as possible. I wish I spoke better French.

We are about to part company, he is intent on heading to the "Sud" I wanted to get away to the north, to try to reach the channel. I show him my escape map. He points to our position, as far as I can tell we are about ten miles behind the French lines, as they had stood this morning.

The Frenchman, I think he said his name was Lewy, so I guess that's what I should call him, Lewy eventually gets me to understand that there was another, very small airfield that some of their planes are using about ten kilometres further south. He is not in a good way and I can see he needs a doctor urgently: Since I don't really fancy my chances of getting across thirty or more miles of German-controlled France, Lewy and I head south together.

We were lucky, we got a lift for over half the distance in a Post-Bus. I am amazed to find something as simple as this charabanc going about its normal activities just a few miles from a German armoured column. On the other hand, I suddenly realise, their armour was heading away from here and charging towards Paris.

I eventually carry Lewy to the gate at the other airfield late afternoon. It is still active. Lewy is whisked off to see the Medic and get his crushed and broken arm sorted out. I am taken to see the Senior Officer, I am pleased to see he is a pilot too, some common ground.

"So, Flight Lieutenant Forntern," he struggled with my name as much as I did with the French names. "What happened that you arrive on my Airfield, with a badly injured man?" His English puts my French to shame, but I try to use as many words as I know.

"Ce matin, ma flight de Spitfires est jumped by les Boches."

"This morning, your Spitfire section was surprised by the Boches, please continue in English. That way we only have to translate things once." Educated and polite, some of the French Officer Class are a cut above.

I describe the brief dog fight and my emergency landing, finding Lewy, the arrival of the Germans and our lucky escape.

"What are your plans from here?" I can see that the French Commander is deeply worried.

"I have to get back to England somehow."

"If what we have both seen from the air were to remain unchanged, you would have to travel west of Paris to reach the British sector and the Germans are moving fast." From the air, the comparatively junior French officer had seen what the Generals would not admit. There was nothing left to stop the Panzers, apart from German High Command.

"The easiest way for me to get back

would be to fly." I am frustrated and tired.

"Then that is what you will do."

"Sorry, Sir. How?" I am confused, what is the man proposing?

"Tomorrow, our three planes will take off and fly north. We will bomb and strafe anything we see on route and land at Bethune, my group Headquarters. I have no more fuel reserves and very little ordnance; this is a satellite base. Your Spitfire is probably still burning on our main airfield."

That was the plan then. I was to get a ride north in a French bomber. The ground crew would evacuate towards Reims, taking my friend Lewy along for further treatment.

I dined with the French pilots that night. The conversation was stilted and very shallow. I resolved to set about learning to speak French properly. These guys were going to risk their lives to help me. There was no option to just follow orders, rather than act on their own initiative. The last set of orders had come through two days earlier; before the Panzers had crossed the border into France.

The next morning, the majority of the ground crew march out of the gate, preceded by the ambulance carrying Lewy and a couple of other wounded airmen, including the rear gunner, who I am to replace on this flight.

We line up, the engines come up to power and we are off. The last of the three aircraft are hardly off the ground, than the last of the men on the ground are climbing into trucks, to follow after the marching men.

The flight to Bethune is, undoubtedly, the scariest of my life. Normally I am in control of the plane, I will never get used to having someone else flying me, facing backwards, especially not in combat. We fly low, very low, in a loose formation, until we get spotted by a group of Me 109s. We scatter, dropping our bombs to increase our speed. The 109s must have been low on fuel and break off the pursuit fairly quickly.

Then we run into a raid by RAF Blenheim bombers, not a problem in itself, but the anti-aircraft guns are already in action as we come into sight. I never want to face flak at low altitude again. You have no room to move, you have no height to lose and if you try to climb, losing speed and exposing the underside of the aircraft to the guns, is not an option. Never again will I allow my fighter colleagues to insult bomber crews. Straight and level, down a predictable path, towards a known target while hundreds of Germans hurl tons of explosives at the aircraft; that takes real courage.

Eventually, I find my way to an RAF base. Chaos reigns here too. Communication lines are severely disrupted, they have no idea where to find my squadron. In fact, apart from the two Hurricanes being refuelled and re-armed, no one knows the whereabouts of any part of Fighter Command; other than they would turn up from time to time when the Blenheims need them. I manage to locate one of the Hurricane pilots, while he was grabbing a coffee.

"Do you know where 612 Squadron are based now?" I ask.

"Are they in England?" He replies.

"When I took off yesterday, they were down the road a bit, near Amiens."

"When we took off from Manston this morning, Amiens was still our side of the frontline, but only just!" He shakes his head slightly. "If I were you, old chap, I'd not bother to look on this side of the water. Head home and get redeployed from there!" He finishes his drink and starts to jog towards his aircraft.

"Good luck!" I shout at his disappearing figure.

"And you, old chap! And you!" He calls back.

"Attack Alarm! Attack Alarm! Action stations!" The tannoy squawks. The pilot sprints for his Hurricane. I dive for a trench. When I look over the parapet a few minutes later, the two fighters are streaking north, at ground level, as fast as their Merlin engines could drag them.

We escape that attack, a convoy of retreating Belgian soldiers, less than a mile away, taking the hit.

Just after lunch, the announcement is made, the base is to be evacuated. The remaining aircraft are to leave at dusk, destination England. The armourers and electrical wizards are to be flown out too. The rest of the ground crew, mainly catering and air defence gunners are to leave by road under cover of darkness.

Ten days after the Germans crossed the borders, I spend the late evening in the Officer's Mess at Northolt, in the company of some of the bomber pilots. A squabble breaks out between a couple of the chaps over assembling for Church Parade. It is quickly defused when the Mess staff pointed out the date on the newspapers, Monday 20th May 1940.

Edward Yeoman

France 1940 - 5

I am officially a Prisoner of War, although I am being repatriated, as they call it. The truth is, I am no longer capable of using a gun, I am no longer a threat, I cannot work in a factory, if they continue to hold me, I would just be a burden. I am being freed as a symbol of the magnanimous nature of the occupying forces.

With my left arm still in a cast, a few Francs of back pay, my discharge papers, a permit to travel and a ticket for trains to Béziers in my pocket, the Germans opened the gate and let me walk away from the camp. Behind me, several thousand faces jealously follow my progress down the road.

I should be jealous of them, they are fit enough, strong enough and whole enough that the Germans want to keep them. I am the one being discarded. Broken beyond future use.

I am not. This was the pact I made with the devil. The exchange I had offered up while trapped under that wrecked aircraft. My left arm for my freedom.

The journey to Béziers took several days. The railways were not fully staffed, many workers have fled to the safety of the south with their families. Others have died, killed in air attacks while working or running. In the early morning, I hand my discharge papers to the same *Armée de L'Air* Recruiting Officer who had signed me up, when I was cold, hungry and broke, back in the winter of 1938.

"Well, Monsieur Verdier, Thank you for your sacrifice. you are now free from your service. Good luck!"

From the front door of the office building, I can only see one path. The way back to Perinac, Hélène and our daughter. I hope it will be safe, I have nowhere else to shelter while my crushed arm heals. While I hope Henri is safe, held a prisoner in the North, I do not know what my future will hold if he returns to the farm.

I have been warned by the surgeons that talk of my arm 'healing' is a bit optimistic. The bones will grow back together and that will stop the pain occurring every time my arm or hand moves. There is no chance of my hand moving in response to my commands, they say, the crushed bones will all fuse making flexing impossible. I am going to have to discover ways of tending the vines with one hand and a stick. I thank God and The Devil that it was my left arm that has been crippled.

It soon becomes very clear that there is no hero's welcome waiting for a wounded soldier home from the war. Backs are turned to me as I pass. I am overcharged for the *petite dejeuner* of bread, jam and coffee I buy to give me strength for the walk ahead. I can understand. Friends and relatives have not come home yet, some will never be coming home and we, the soldiers, have let the French people down. I know, because I have seen the bravery and sacrifice of the individual man at arms, the failure was at a higher level in the military and political structure of the nation.

As I walk the thirty kilometres, along hot, dusty roads, to Perinac; thoughts float through my mind. The slow response of the Generals to the declaration of war. The lack of modern weapons, and the time to train with them, in thirty-nine. The Bréguet was a fine plane but they arrived too late and there were too few. We had been able to drill with aircraft all night long, hoisting bombs into their cradles, avoiding the door frames, moving boxes of ammunition in and out. We, the ground team had our roles down pat. Meanwhile, the pilots had only managed a few hours a day. They had no chance to explore the tactical use of the plane, it was all theory. Rather poor theory as it turned out on day one. I suspect it was the same with the new anti-tank rifles and all the other kit being rushed into service.

These are the type of thoughts that keep me company as I walk along the dusty road towards Perinac. The heat grows in intensity as the sun rises higher in the sky. I stop at a small café; it is almost deserted; Madame dishes me up a bowl of a thin stew of vegetables with a few shreds of chicken. I sit inside the café and watch the old men coming in and drinking, a coffee, a beer or glass of wine before heading home for their lunch. Then an old boy with his filthy, faded, old beret enters and orders a pastis and le menu.

He looks across the small room at me.

"Veteran?" He grunts by way of conversation.

"Yes." I reply, "I was in the north when the Boches attacked. Many of our compatriots died, slaughtered trying to stop their tanks."

"It was the same during the offensive of 1918," He coughed and spat. "Except it was the storm troopers we feared, not tanks." He eats his stew, slowly and vanishes back out into the heat.

I finish my beer and the pichet of water. I leave a few coins on the table and walk towards the door.

"When will they be back? The rest of the men?" Almost the first words the hostess had uttered.

"A few like me, soon. Most will be used as workers by the Germans until the war ends. Others, lots of others: never." I walk out into the heat and pick up my journey.

I walk along the road shaded by the trees planted over a hundred years earlier to protect marching men of another army, in an earlier war. The fields that surround me planted with serried rows of vines, some tended and neat; most, untidy, unpruned and ill-cared for. Where I used to see men labouring the vines far away from the roads, there are none. As I pass the farmers' cottages a few rows of grapes are being tended by the same women and children that labour in the vegetable plots or caring for the livestock.

Old men bent and weathered by fifty, sixty or even more summers of labour, are back at work. They carry impossible loads across the fields. Loads, that they should be sat criticising their sons for not taking up to the vines ages ago. This is a country stripped of its workforce. A way of life struggling to survive with the loss of a whole generation. The too old passing their knowledge and rusty skills on to children too young, too immature and who have yet to acquire the strength they will need. Knowledge and skills that could be so quickly lost before the youngsters realise that they need to understand and practice them while there are still people who they can ask for advice.

It is late afternoon when I crest that last hill and can see Perinac spread out before me.

It is no longer the neatly trimmed village I remember seeing from this vantage point in the years before the war came. I turn off the main road onto the track that follows a fold in the land towards the farm.

As I get closer, I can see that the vines are untended, unpruned and clogged with weeds. The vegetable garden looks better tended though and a dozen chickens are scratching around in a pen. A young girl, dressed in a dull brown dress that has seen better days, sits in the porchway playing with a crude wooden doll. I know it to be crude, I had fashioned it during my last stay in Perinac.

As I get closer, the youngster becomes aware of my approach, startled she dives through the door. "Maman, Maman there is a man coming!"

I am staggered by Hélène's appearance; she is much thinner, she looks exhausted, her hair loose and unkempt, her clothes soiled and stained and her hand clenches a large carving knife. Defiance blazes in her eyes, then she recognises me and drops the knife.

My arm flares with pain as she embraces me, sobbing onto my shoulder. "Louis, Louis you are alive, thank the gods you are alive." Our daughter stands in the doorway, shyly looking on, worried for her mother.

Minutes pass and I am on the point of passing out. I wobble on my feet and Hélène realises there is something wrong.

"Your arm!"

"When it heals, I will still be able to hold you, my sweet."

Over a glass of wine and a plain omelette I tell her of my time under the wrecked aircraft, of the help from the English flyer, who I hope is safe back in his home country, and the German NCO, who I hope has been granted a swift and painless death. I tell her of my time as a prisoner and my release because I am no longer fit to work for the Boches!

Then I ask the question, I need to know and dread the answer to, "Henri?"

"He is missing, presumed dead, officially. I don't expect him back. I got a letter from one of the Sergeants in the Regiment. They had all swapped addresses of their nearest and dearest in the hope that news might get home." Her face was cold and emotionless, I had seen expressionless faces like hers on fellow POWs as they tried to avoid seeing the unforgettable.

"Not good news?" Her face came back to life.

"Henri will not return to Perinac in this life. They were part of a defensive line near Arras when the Panzers turned on them. The anti-tank gun failed and a Panzer drove over the foxhole Henri's section were sheltering in, three times, collapsing it, turning it into a grave for the men hiding in the earth. His comrades didn't have time to try to recover the bodies, so, that is where Henri will spend eternity."

I pulled Hélène towards me holding her tight with my good arm.

"It could have been so much worse. It could be him stood here and you, crushed, in a muddy hole, far away in the north." Hélène smiles through her tears.

The bastard that I am, I am glad to hear of my rival's destruction. Tomorrow, the first day of September, will be the day I start to build a new life for me, my very good friend, Hélène, and our daughter, Sandrine.

The last day of August 1940

France 1940 - 6

France surrendered as we headed west. Before we ground to a halt for the Armistice, we had almost reached Bordeaux. I have never been so far west in all my life, although one of the officers claims he was on a boat west of here when he was going to Spain in 1937. He makes these claims all the time, whatever anybody has done; he has done it better.

"Damn officers! If they aren't pushing us around, 'do this, not that way the other way, fools', then they are boasting about having breakfast with the Führer."

"It is not as if many of them have seen any more combat than Emil, here, has anyway!" An anonymous voice from the huddle of enlisted men, gathered around, sharing a smoke.

"I hope that it means I don't see any more combat. I want to go home with both my balls!"

"Unteroffizer Brunnig!"

"Hauptmann!" Oh God, he was listening. I snap to attention.

"Did I hear you admitting to cowardice, refusing to fight the enemies of the German people?"

"Nein, Herr Hauptman! I was expressing my wish that now we have demonstrated the armed power of the Reich, that all the enemies of the German people, will lay down their arms at the feet of the Führer." I remember that from one of the lectures we sat through in the Hitler Youth. That I could remember anything of those talks was a miracle. We were teenage boys and had different interests, mainly concerning the girls in the row in front of us.

"A very smart answer Brunnig, be careful!"

This is one Junior Officer who is not going to like his billet. I had my orders to report to the *Rathaus,* or as the writing on the wall, below the flag of France, said '*Mairie'*, I was assigned to translate for the Billeting Officer. We have to find and assign suitable accommodation for the Officers. I suspect that the braggard might find himself living in less comfort than the others. Such is the petty power of an Unteroffizer Translator.

The following morning, I write the Hauptmann's name next to a chicken farmer's address. Cockerels crowing at five o'clock should ensure he is awake ready for early duty.

I didn't get time to find myself a comfortable billet though. Two days later, I am on my way to central Bordeaux. It appears that my status as a translator has been noted by someone in High Command. I am to join the staff of the Port Kommandant as his official translator and I am to become a Sergeant, a necessary promotion for the level of classified documents I will have access too.

"Dear Helga," I write. "I am as far west as either of us has ever wanted to go." That might get past the censors. "We are all safe and capitulation of the enemies of the German people means we have no further opportunity to garner greater glory. I have been rewarded for my skill with the language of our defeated foes and I am now your husband. Sergeant Emil Brunnig."

It was all rubbish, what I wanted to say was, "I am safe. People are no longer shooting at me (or dropping bombs on me!) and I have had a pay rise. Please write to me, I haven't had a letter for over a month!"

*****

There is a mountain of work for me to do, not least helping the Port Kommandant to get the correct French union officials to take control of the docks. The less cooperative find that they are to be transferred to other duties. The men we identified as communists were to be sent for re-education in Germany.

By the time we started getting reports of Communist activity from stool pigeons we had placed, we were too late to immediately arrest the Reds. Most of the people in question had discovered that they wanted to seek relocation for family or other reasons. I wonder if it was the way I phrased the Kommandant's question. The one about how we need all of the senior men to identify any communists in the workforce; so that we could deport them to the east. I suppose it is a bit wordy. Such is the petty power of a Sergeant translator.

Initially, my work is focussed on getting the port open for business. It is a vital opening to the west for Germany. Important war cargo could be brought from Africa and the Americas could be landed in Bordeaux and taken by rail to the industrial areas of Europe, without the need to run the English guns and aircraft in a dash up the English Channel under the cover of darkness.

Then, I receive new orders, originating from ReichFührer Goering's office. I am to report to a meeting in a room above the storerooms of a famous wine house. Bordeaux is full of famous wine names. It is also full of bottles, barrels and cellars of wine. Good wine, wine that would grace the tables of party officials, SS officers and generals. Millions of bottles of wine, thousands of kilometres from the Fatherland. The powers that be in Germany want these wines and are prepared, I thought surprisingly, to pay. This meeting is the start of the process of negotiating the terms for one of the first purchases.

Yes, the price was low. Yes, the value of the currency was being manipulated but people got paid. Which is more than could be said of any promissory orders made by the British wine trade! They were in no position to pay for the wine they had ordered back in the spring. We are also in a position to take delivery of large quantities of wine, whereas the blockade by the British Navy makes deliveries to other export markets much harder.

It seems that my work was to someone important's satisfaction. I was reassigned again; I am now on the staff of the Bordeaux Weinführer. No change in rank this time, but a definite step up the prestige ladder. I have a new billet, a shared room on the second floor of what used to be a commercial travellers' hotel; located on the edge of the wine quarter. Seven of us from the Weinführer's office share the four double rooms and the bathroom, as the senior-ranking enlisted man in the group, the second bed in my room is one that is left unoccupied.

I imagine the letter I want to write to Helga, "I have a room to myself in the hotel. We have an account with the Café on the ground floor. He overcharges the Wehrmacht for our food and undercharges us for the wine we drink. Please come and visit me!"

No chance that would get past the censor's office. I know with absolute certainty it would be a short cut to the Punishment Division. So why would I do that when life in Bordeaux is good.

All in all, 1940 has been a good year for me. As an infantryman, I rode in trucks and on the back of tanks right across France, seldom having to march more than a kilometre or two. I have kept my rifle clean, oiled and ready to shoot at all times, but I haven't had to fire it once. I have seen enemy action from a distance but was only ever fired on by my own countrymen. Just for keeping my nose clean and learning French at school, I have been promoted, twice.

War is hell.

The last day of October 1940.

France 1944

The fruit has set on the vines; I hope we can find enough workers to help with the picking this year. The Germans had promised us some Italian prisoners as labour but with the invasion taking place in the north, will they have the time and manpower to move POWs to and from the camps? We had been promised this help by the Germans after the Italians had surrendered last autumn, but none had arrived in time. This year it would be helpful to have some experienced pickers even if they are Italian.

"I hope they work harder than the hired help we used to have on this farm," Hélène had joked. "He used to spend hours just lounging around, lazing under the olive trees, distracting me from my work!"

"I am sure it was mutual; you have the looks and the figure to distract any red-blooded man for most tasks." I had replied. I wasn't joking either.

One of the advantages of having areas of vines out of production is we have space for a few extra chickens and rows of vegetables hidden away from the German inspectors. The Boches arrive from time to time and demand we supply up to half the food and wine we grow to the Reich. They pay but only at derisory, low prices. We are all trying to hide a little bit of extra food. A neighbour has a small herd of billy goats, that he had allegedly slaughtered, you can't milk billy goats and he is a cheesemaker. In the good years, we used to have a feast of kid goat each spring. Now we get a little goat meat every so often, as long as we have something to exchange. We have eggs to trade for little extras.

An attempt by another villager to hide a couple of dairy cows was uncovered when they were overheard mooing by one of the inspectors. The farmer managed to escape punishment by claiming he had been raising them to be offered to the German army, so that he could keep more of his vegetable harvest. The family nearly starved, only just surviving the hungry months as they lost the cattle and most of the production of their vegetable garden; at least the father was still on the land to plant begged seeds for the following year.

For a couple of years, many of us had kept pigs hidden away in caves. Now there wasn't enough food waste to feed them. They might taste good but they need a lot of food if they are going to grow. People were now preferring to eat their vegetables unpeeled rather than cutting off up to third of a potato to feed to a pig. The caves we had used as underground pigsties were now filled wine that had escaped the audit.

It was tough for us; in the big towns and cities, it must have been incredibly hard to get by these past four years.

I lean on my hoe; I am clearing the weeds between the rows of our best vines. Yes, our vines, I married the widow, Hélène Menton, last year when the authorities accepted the evidence that Private Henri Menton had been killed at the Battle of Arras in 1940. I was now the owner of the Menton family farm. My wife, as the only relative apart from his daughter, had inherited the property and upon our marriage, it had passed to me. Which explains why I am out here, working in the blistering early afternoon heat, instead of being tucked up in the arms of my lover.

"Sandrine!" I hear Hélène calling out from the back door.

I wipe the sweat from my forehead and look up to see my daughter carrying a bag of food up to the chickens.

"Yes, Mamma," she calls back down the hill.

"Don't try to carry too many eggs, call for me if there are too many for you to fetch!"

"I will, Mamma!"

Wisdom and resilience beyond their

years is something that all the local children seem to have. The adolescent kids I had seen being shown how to work the grapes just three summers ago are now farmers. The older men are now worn-out husks, pottering in the vegetable gardens offering advice, wanted or not, to the teenagers doing a man's job, every day before and after school.

At nine years of age, although Sandrine is as skinny as a bean, her dress, patched and worn as it is, is tight to her slight frame. I hope that we have enough eggs to get one of Verve Lavigne's dresses when she passes away. I hear people expect she will be gone before the week is out. Hélène will then have enough cloth to make our daughter a new outfit.

Yes, the rest of the villagers think I am wonderful, taking on not only a widow but her late husband's child and treating her as my own. I just hope that one day soon the war will be over and Hélène and I can stop being careful and allow nature to give Sandrine a brother or sister.

I want to be able to take my beautiful, kind, generous wife up to the stand of olive trees and spend an afternoon making babies. That would be heaven, after four years of counting days and the whip-it out and wipe it approach that, between them, have served us pretty well for four years. I am tired of the stress and worry, it shows in my performance, I am barely any more use than Henri was some days.

There are rumours, someone in town has a radio and can hear the BBC news, that Caen is about to fall to the British. We heard that Cherbourg was taken a few days ago, it looks like the British and Americans are in France to stay this time. I also heard that the resistance fighters are being supplied with guns and explosives, ready for some sort of operation.

Could the end be approaching?

In a sudden flash, I realise that it was ten years ago today that Hélène and I made baby Sandrine.

The last day of June 1944!

Edward Yeoman

30,000 Feet 1944

The channel, several miles below us, is crowded with ships dashing back and forth. The smoke of battle rises from a town I can see dead ahead of my Spitfire. Below me, the Typhoons we were escorting are preparing for their low-level swoop looking for Jerry tanks and other strong points as targets for their cannon and rockets. After the Typhoons have turned for home, I'll let the boys have some fun. I'll take the ducklings home; I'm not supposed to be here in the first place.

"Blue-three to White Chief"

"White Chief, go ahead Blue-three."

"White Chief, there was a bandit at my three o'clock."

"Was, Blue-three?"

"Yes Chief, the Yanks got him, he dived away with his engine smoking."

That was it, over the past year the mighty Luftwaffe has sort of disappeared. That was why I had decided it would be safe enough to overlook the orders forbidding me flying on combat missions. I will claim there was no risk of combat and I was on a training flight to keep my hours up if anybody asks.

"White Chief to White Wing, go and have fun boys, I'll see the children across the road."

It wasn't as if the Typhoons weren't capable of looking after themselves now that they had shed their loads. At low-level, the 'Tiffy' was more than a match to all types of German fighter aircraft and "We could probably take your Spitfire without breaking into a sweat!" As the indignant Typhoon Squadron Leader pointed out in my earphones.

Over the coast, we part company and I turned for home. I am completing my cockpit checks and I am about to lower the undercarriage when pandemonium breaks out on the airwaves. Suddenly, I see why. A Foche-wulf 190 is beating up the airfield. He may have snuck across the Channel, but he wasn't going back. I angled the nose down and my finger hovered over the button that would send a stream of 20mm shells into the attacker.

"Who needs a Typhoon? Even at this sort of altitude!" I congratulate my Spitfire, as I look around to make sure the Foche is down and nothing else is shaping up for a bite at me,

If he was lucky, he might be able to walk away from that crash, I decide as I over-fly the crash site. The German pilot had hit the ground with most of his left-wing missing and slid across a field of cereal crops, losing speed and the right-wing on the way. There, it was my first kill in over a year. I expect it will be my last. They don't let Group Captains do a lot of flying.

My brother-in-law William, Lord Denham, had been impressed when I got the third thick bar on my epaulettes, as a Wing Commander, he had thrown a champagne reception at Denham Hall. I didn't ask how he knew before I did or how I got a five-day pass at the same time. William's war was very different from mine. While he had been at the forefront of those celebrations, he was conspicuous by his absence as I gained the fourth bar and a rank equivalent to a full Colonel.

Instead of champagne and five days in the luxury of Heather's family home, we had opened a bottle of claret and shared a piece of steak. The butcher had dropped this into Heather's shopping bag, in place of the sausages for this week's ration, on hearing about my promotion.

The war had been a tough time for me, like most men of my generation, I had lost good friends. Giles de Urville, the happy homosexual, I had shared any number of adventures with as an undergraduate, and after we came down from Cambridge, had died in his burning tank in some god-forsaken part of the Libyan desert. Johnnie Mays would never drive his Bentley again; his Lancaster had failed to return from a raid in '43. Then there were my Squadron colleagues. Too many for me to want to remember. Men and boys, who had taken off alongside me but never came back. Besides the dead, there are a large number of physical and mentally damaged men with whom I have served. The burned, the blinded, the amputees, the drinkers, the addicts and the nervously exhausted were almost beyond count.

Several times, when I had been on the point of breaking, it was Heather who was my anchor in the world of sanity. No longer the wild party girl of the 1930s she was the serious-minded District Welfare Officer for the Land Army. She was responsible for the pastoral wellbeing of several dozen young women, town girls in the main, called up to work on the farms; girls who became homesick or suffered from bullying. Young women who fell pregnant or were deserted by boyfriends. Women bereaved, widowed or orphaned by bombing and combat. She had built a shell around the inner Heather, only when we were alone together could either of us let down our defences and cry on each other's shoulders.

There was a note on my desk, "Mrs Thornton called at 11:45. She asked if you could call her back, please. She will be at home all day." There was a scrawl at the bottom of the page, the signature of the WAAF

Writer who had taken the message.

I walked across the corridor from my room to the admin office. I showed the note to the WAAF Sergeant in charge of the section. "Who took this message?" I asked.

"That would be ACW Smith." She pointed to a petite girl with dark hair.

"May I have a quick word with her, please, Sergeant? Outside."

"Sir." She beckoned the worried-looking Aircraftwoman over, Smith got to her feet and hurried over. The youngster stopped in front of me and saluted.

"I'd like a quick word about this message. Nothing bad." I could see her starting to fret, what did the new 'Groupie' want with her? I opened the door and guided her out into the corridor.

"Sir?" The young ACW stood at attention.

"Stand easy, Smith, I just wanted to ask about this note. Am I right to assume it was you who spoke to Mrs Thornton?"

"Yes, Sir."

"Good, I just want a little background.

Did she say anything else? Or was that the total conversation?"

"Mrs Thornton asked if you were available to talk to her. I said you had duties that prevented you from coming to the phone just then. She said "Right-ho, leave a message for him to call as soon as possible, I'll be home all day." I wrote the note, read it back to her, she thanked me and rang off."

"How did she sound?"

"Sir?"

"You know, did she sound excited? Happy? Sad?"

"She sounded sort of 'normal' but of course I don't know how Mrs Thornton normally sounds. If you'll excuse me saying, Sir."

"That is fine, Smith. Thank you for your help. Oh, by the way, in future, don't salute me unless you have your hat on."

That hadn't helped much. Heather had a special 'not-in-front-of-the-servants' voice that hid all emotions. I picked up the phone and placed the call, was it going to be more sad news or for once a little good news.

Heather answered on the third ring,

"Hello." The 'servants' voice. It was news she didn't want to leak out before she had told me. I brace myself for some more bad news.

"Hello, Darling, you left a message for me to call you?"

"Yes, I did. Daddy!"

The war has been hell, but over the Channel this afternoon I had seen the beginning of the end. The tide had changed, today was the last day of my flying career and my first as a family man….

The last day of June 1944.

Edward Yeoman

Bordeaux 1944

Confusion reigns in this sector, rumours fly around that the Allies have landed in about four places between La Rochelle and Bordeaux, except that nobody has heard any explosions. Even the submarine pens have escaped attack for a couple of weeks.

Even if there is no truth in the rumours, most of the senior officers are running about like headless chickens, sorting out their personal evacuation plans. Not an hour passes when I don't receive a request to ship a few private cases of wine back to the Fatherland. I doubt that wine is all these cases will be filled with.

"I'm sorry Sir, but all the wagons are filled with essential material for the next few weeks. I could get small packages squeezed in, provided the shipping orders are signed by one of the General Staff."

I am offered bribes and I could have found space for many of these extra shipments; one day the caller would be at a desk in Gestapo headquarters. The following morning, I'd be on my way East to join a Punishment Division or, if I was lucky, in front of a firing squad.

The Boss is out, in confidential

conversations with some of the producers who used to do the special bottling for us. I imagine it is a when this is all over and things get back to normal, I'll remember who my friends were, type conversation.

According to one of the things I have read, there was a thriving industry selling 'not Bordeaux' before we arrived. I have seen it suggested, that even as early as the turn of the century twice as much fine Bordeaux was being drunk as the region produced. So maybe that batch of Minervois that went East in Bordeaux bottles, carrying Bordeaux labels for the private cellar of Reichsmarschall Göring is part of a historic tradition. The Boss doesn't have a lot of time for 'Fat Herman.' Which is quite brave of him, men have died for less!

Still, with the Boss out of the way, I have got time to read Helga and the children's latest letter. Even the bits that she has written in normal ink are quite depressing. The children being off school and that the Bergmanns had moved in suggested a lot more damage from bombing than when I was last home.

I hold the paper over my desk lamp. After a few minutes, more writing appears brown against the white. The news is not good. The railway at Offenburg had been subject to a big raid a few months back. Lots of people had been bombed out and moved into new neighbourhoods. Some bombs had fallen near our house, the gas had been cut off for several days.

I thank the gods that our home is still intact and that it is summer and the gas is less important than in winter. I read on.

"The ration has been cut again, less butter, cheese and meat."

At least she hadn't mentioned the bread ration. Then there was the sad news about our friends.

"Karl Weber and Wolfgang Schmidt, two of our comrades in the Hitler Youth, had been killed on the Eastern Front and young Max Hessler, our audience that wonderful day you were on leave, has been lost in Italy."

The news of my friends and that young scallywag made me feel desperately sad.

"I am well, but we are all hungry for most of the day. I look forward to you coming home and bringing peace and plenty. All my love, Helga."

As I am reading this tragic missive for the third or fourth time, there is an outbreak of shouting and the sound of running feet out in the corridor. I just have time to stuff the incriminating paper inside my tunic as the office door is thrown open.

We are standing to alongside several battered cattle wagons in the rail marshalling yards, when a dozen trucks with SS markings arrive. We take up positions with our rifles at the ready as the tailgates are dropped and men fall from the dark interiors. The SS men use clubs and rifle butts to chase these men, many already wounded or beaten into the railway cattle-cars.

The railway wagons, crowded with two hundred maybe two hundred and fifty men, are barred and locked. The SS men climb back into their trucks and bump off the way they came in.

A man, a thickset, blonde-haired thug, gets out of a staff car that has arrived from somewhere during the excitement. The Leutnant, who had pulled us out of the Headquarters, marches towards the vehicle, stops and salutes the Gestapo man. In return, he is given a sealed envelope. Our orders no doubt.

"Sergeant Brunnig!" The officer bawled.

"Mein Herr!" I respond as I hurry to where he was opening the papers. 'Christ!' I think. 'I must be the ranking NCO! I hope this is an easy task.'

Easy it was and rather brutal. We were to stand guard until a locomotive arrives and takes the prisoners away. As a French speaker, I am to read the next part of the orders, out loud to the troops and the prisoners.

"By order of the Occupying Forces of the Third Reich. You are detained as enemies of the state. Any attempt at escape will result in you being shot and returned to the railcar from which you escaped. Food and water will be provided at your next stop."

The rest of the orders detail how the six-man guard is to be positioned around the train and how often we are to change shift. The initial six men take up their assigned positions. The rest of us seek shelter from the burning June sun.

Occasionally, there are groans of pain and shouts of defiance from the train. Nobody tries to escape so nobody gets shot. Six hours later the locomotive arrives, pulling a flak carriage and a passenger car full of Romanian SS. The cattle trucks are attached and the train pulls off.

We are ordered back into our trucks and ride back to Headquarters.

"Jews, do you think?" Someone asks.

"Yeah, Jews and Commies!" A heavy reply.

"And the fucking Resistance!" Someone near the tailgate spat…

The last day of June 1944 and war is shit!

France 1946

I am gasping for breath, holding myself upright while I wait for Mme Leclerc to gather the tools of her trade. Hélène is in labour; I have left her in the care of Sandrine, our eleven-year-old daughter. It only takes a few minutes and *la sage-femme,* the closest thing we have to a qualified midwife in the village, is hurrying along beside me as we retrace my dash to her door.

Life in Perinac is easier than it had been during the war, at least we get to choose what we sell and what we keep for ourselves. We are no longer starving, although nothing else has changed much. Our clothes and boots are old and worn. The tools and machines we work with are battered and much repaired, but we are alive, we are safe and one day… one day!

I suspect it happened on the evening that we had our first *Fête des Vendanges,* celebrating bringing in the grape harvest since before the Germans arrived. The whole village had partied late into the night, roasting one of the concealed pigs and drinking a little of our hidden wine stocks. In truth, we drank more than a little wine. As the night had drawn to a close it had turned into the kind of pagan festival our traditional *fêtes* are based upon. Mme Leclerc was experiencing her busiest week in many years.

"Papa, Papa, quickly! The baby has come!" Sandrine is jumping up and down with excitement as I hurry into the house. The *sage-femme* pushes past and up the stairs to the bedroom. Sandrine is hanging on to my arm.

"Papa, it is a little boy! I helped Mama when it was coming, I held him!"

"Well done, Sandrine. I am sure you helped your Mama a lot!" I have only been gone for an hour and I have gained a son!

"Mama, wanted you. She called for you lots of times, I held her hand, so she knew I was there. Then I helped the baby out, he has black hair!"

Mme Leclerc returned to the kitchen. "All is well. I will prepare some soup for the new mother. Go up and meet your son, Louis. Sandrine, you stay here and help me find everything."

I enter the bedroom; my beautiful Hélène is propped up on a couple of pillows her dark hair still damp with perspiration and her face flushed. In her arms, she holds a tiny bundle. She lifts it up for me to take. A shock of dark hair and gentle snuffling noises. It's my son, our son.

"Louis, meet Henri."

Gingerly, I take the bundle from her, I feel awkward, initially, my damaged arm makes it difficult. With the bundle cradled safely, I pull back the blanket and gaze on the scrunched up pink face. His eyes open momentarily, grey, like mine and like his sister's; in that instant, I know I that I am holding the most precious thing in the world in my arms.

"Hello, Henri. Welcome to the world." Hélène and I had talked about the name. We had agreed that we would call him after Hélène's late husband. I know that sounds strange but, old Henri had not been a bad man. He had been a good husband to Hélène. His only real failing was as a stud. With hindsight, I even suspect that he had known he was not Sandrine's real father. Grey eyes like hers and mine are rare. The farm he had owned and run had become our home. We felt we owed him and this way, one day, the farm would become 'Henri's Farm' once more.

There is a tap on the door, Mme Leclerc pokes her head around the doorframe. "Sandrine is looking after the soup; it will be ready in a little while. I have to go; I hope this year's *Fête des Vendanges* is a little more restrained. I can't cope with delivering the same number of babies next June!"

I follow the midwife to the door of our

cottage and hand her a small bundle of francs, which she slips into her pocket, uncounted. We all pay her what we can afford, nobody short-changes her. It is a matter of honour.

"Do not forget Sandrine, I know she not officially your daughter, she is a clever girl and needs to be reassured that she is still part of this family."

"Officially or not, Sandrine is my daughter."

"I have known that since I first looked you in the eye, Louis Verdier, the very first time. Just don't let the excitement of a new son push her out of your affection."

"Thank you for the reminder, Mme Leclerc. You are truly a *sage-femme.* I hope the next call is as simple as this one."

"*Merci, M Verdier, a bientôt!*" She hurried off; her next delivery is calling.

Back indoors, I help Sandrine ladle the soup into three bowls and cut a few chunks of bread. We put the bowls, spoons and bread on a tray, which Sandrine carries carefully up the stairs. I follow with two chairs from the kitchen table.

In the bedroom, we arrange the two chairs, either side of the bed and then with

Henri nuzzling his mother's breast we eat our first meal as a family of four.

"This is an important day," Hélène pauses and glances at me, I guess what is coming and nod my agreement. "Twelve years ago your Papa and I made you, Sandrine, and now your brother, our second child has arrived on that anniversary."

It is the last day of June 1946, probably the happiest day of my life.

Edward Yeoman

England 1946

I am glad it is all over. Maybe now, we can start to enjoy the peace. Heather and I have endured the pain of the war for a year longer than many. There have been times when I think that it was only our love for young Giles that kept us going.

Our son is named for the man who had brought Heather and me together, back in those heady inter-war years in Cambridge. My outrageously camp friend, who had died in a blazing tank nearly five years ago. Somehow, even at eighteen months old, our son seems to have inherited his namesake's larger than life personality.

Heather and I had made it safely through the last year of the war. My final 'victory' had also marked my last flight. For the remaining months of the conflict, I had flown a desk. I didn't even ask to take part in the victory fly-past. Heather and I were too busy with her brother, William, Lord Denton.

William's war had been different from mine. I had known this quite early on in the conflict. It was obvious when he had organised the champagne bash to celebrate my promotion to Wing Commander. His non-appearance for the celebration of my next promotion had been another piece of evidence.

It transpired, when he finally came home, he had been in occupied France. Deep undercover, an SOE liaison with a resistance group based near Lille. He had been helping to organise attacks on the transport network, designed to slow the movement of equipment and reinforcements to the Nazi forces in Northern France. At some stage, he had been betrayed.

Handed to the Gestapo, William had been tortured. Then sent to Berlin for further interrogation and eventually he was sent to the Prince Albrecht Strasse Headquarters for final interrogation and execution. A raid by RAF Bomber Command on Berlin that night had resulted in confusion. Names, cell numbers and destinations got muddled and instead of the firing squad, William was on his way to Buchenwald.

How he had survived until the arrival of the Americans in April 1945 is beyond me. How he had found the strength to carry on afterwards … All I can think of it was his determination to bring his torturers to justice.

He was considered well enough to be nursed at home in September and returned to his family home. It was when we saw him for the first time, that I finally understood man's potential for inhumanity to fellow men.

He had been mutilated. His toes and

fingers had been amputated, His eyelids were missing and his nose had been smashed and then torn apart, spatchcocked. His breathing was restricted by the damage caused by broken ribs ripping his lungs apart. To Heather's distraught reaction to seeing him in this condition, all he had to say was, "I got off lightly, it was much worse for the women." Which scared me stupid.

A few weeks passed, and he was not showing any signs of improvement. Then the investigators from the War Crimes Commission arrived. I was asked, as a family member, to be present while he gave his evidence. As I listened to him giving his evidence for the court, I understood what had kept him alive.

He named the men and women who had broken every bone in his hands and feet, one by one. He gave the name of the doctor who had removed his eyelids. William knew the name of the officer who had signed the order for his toes and fingers to be cut-off joint by joint with a pair of bolt cutters. He identified the SS men who stood masturbating while he was subjected to vile sexual assaults. It sickened me so much that on several occasions I had to demand that the investigators should allow me to escape.

After a couple of weeks, it was over, the questions asked, the names named and the obscenities written down. The investigators went away to write up the statement. William seemed to find some peace. The family lawyer came and went. I was sent for.

"Charles, I want you to promise me a couple of things."

I nod, then realise that he couldn't see me through the dark goggles that protect his eyes. I answer out loud, "I'll try my best."

"Always cautious, that is one of the characteristics that I admire in you, Charles. Never commit until you know what you are committing too."

"I hate breaking promises, William. Especially to people I care about."

"That is why I let you marry my sister. I knew you could be relied on to keep your vows. Therein lies the first promise. I want you to take care of my heirs. You do understand that young Giles will be Lord Denton after me. The lawyers have written to the King, informing him of my dying wish that my nephew will get the title." Adding under his breath, "for what it will be worth."

"Of course, William. Your heir is also my heir remember."

"True!" He laughed, briefly, before it turned to a cough.

'His poor lungs!' I thought.

"The second thing I need you to do is to accept the position of Regent Lord Denton until he comes of age. That will enable you and Heather to live here and manage the upkeep of the old place."

"It would be an honour to fulfil the role, even for a short time."

"The third thing, I want you to be my executor. I want you to do everything you can to protect the house. I have a plan, a list of articles to sell in what order. Will you promise to follow that plan the best you can?"

"Yes, and I will commit as much of my family's money as comes my way to preserving our heir's inheritance."

"From the day I met you, I knew I could rely on you, Charles!"

"I'm not sure about that, I was just one of the undergraduates at a seminar you took."

"February 1934, there were four undergraduates. You shone through." Tension suddenly seems to leave William's body; he sinks back into the pillows. "Thank God I listened to Heather when she begged me to let you stay in the RAF back in '39. None of the other chaps I brought into SOE survived, that is why I had to!"

I was staggered. My brother-in-law had wanted me in SOE and my wife, Heather, had interceded to keep me safe as a fighter pilot. I thought that I had been the one in charge.

A judge from the War Crimes' Court arrived one day in early spring. He and I sat with William while his statement was read into the Court record. Then in mid-April, almost a year to the day that the Americans had liberated Buchenwald, William died, slipping away in the quiet of the night.

Since then the will has been read. The death duties calculated and I have set about selling the assets, in the order that William had planned, to pay the huge bill. Today, though, is a break from these sad duties.

Today, Heather and I get to take young Giles to Sandringham, where the King will present us with the Amended Letters Patent that will enable Giles to inherit the titles William held. A move that has the support of the Labour Government, despite their general dislike of the Peerage system. Like many SOE operatives, William had received no war medals and granting this harmless posthumous wish was considered his reward.

I expect today will be the first and last time I wear my Number 1 uniform, my Best

Blues, complete with my medal ribbon. It seems fitting that they have chosen today, the twelfth anniversary of the day of 'that' party…

The last day of June 1946.

Edward Yeoman

Germany 1946

The war may have ended, but I am still in uniform. On the good side, I am allowed to go home from time to time to see Helga and the children. She tells me the tiny amounts of food that the rations allow is an improvement on what they were entitled to and a huge amount better than what they had physically received in the dying days of the Reich.

I walked most of the way from Bordeaux home, we had trucks for the first leg of the journey. We had been taken south to try to help repulse the landings by the Allies on the Rivera. As we hurried south and east, we were caught in the open by American aircraft. We managed to find shelter in the ditches by the side of the road, but the trucks and all our heavy equipment were destroyed.

We never really got to stand and fight. We retreated throughout the early autumn, falling back towards the Rhine. One morning in early November, I have no idea to this day where we were, we had no orders, no food and preciously little ammunition, we hadn't seen an officer for three days. We found ourselves surrounded by Americans.

As the senior NCO, I order the surrender. This isn't the Eastern Front, our captors are Americans, not Russians. We lay down our rifles and I raise my filthy handkerchief as a white flag.

We are directed to the rear. "About ten miles," the American officer tells us.

An American private, with a Dutch accent, says, "Fünfzehn kilometres!"

Under the guard of two of the Americans, we march south-west, back the way we had retreated along, for four hours. Just after noon, we arrived at a wire enclosure, containing fifty or so of our countrymen. There is water and a little food waiting for us. We settle down to await our fate.

There is a disturbance which attracts my attention in another compound. I immediately recognise the difference. While the men around me are dressed in the field grey uniform of the Wehrmacht, the men in the other pen are in the black or olive uniforms, the SS.

The following morning, we are marched further south and handed over to the French Military Authorities. I have no idea what happened to the SS men, although I hear many are to be put on trial for War Crimes. After what I saw of them, and the Gestapo, in Bordeaux, they have it coming.

We are all questioned by the French, some of the men who marched with our party didn't return from their interrogation. Nobody missed them, nobody could remember seeing them until the day before.

"Typical SS cowards!" Coughed the oldest man in our group. "It was the same in Russia, as soon as things looked bad, there were the 'heroic' SS men, trying to get into Wehrmacht uniforms so they wouldn't be identified." He coughed again before regaining his breath. The wound that had damaged lung had saved him from being sent back east to die.

"Brunnig, Sergeant Brunnig!" A French officer, accompanied by two armed men, was looking for me. I stood up.

"*Ici, Monsieur. Je suis Brunnig*"

"Good, Sergeant Brunnig, you are to report to the Commandant's Office tomorrow at reveille." It looks like I am back to being a translator again.

To this day that is my role in life, translator for the French Occupying Forces. The good news is, I am based in Freiburg im Breisgau. The state of Baden lies within the French sector. As does my home. I am allowed the occasional three- or four-day pass that enables me to travel the sixty kilometres to spend time with my wife and children.

Tonight, we will eat a stew made with the bones I liberated from the kitchen bins behind the Officers' Mess. There may not be a lot of meat on them, but the flavour will make the vegetable stew much more tasty.

While my mother prepares the Sunday lunch and looks after the children, Helga and I go for a walk. It is a rare moment alone. There are six adults and five children in my family home. Both Helga's and my mothers, Herr Lang and the Bergmanns and the Bergmann's two grandchildren, in addition to Helga and our children. There was very little privacy at home, which is why we walk.

The town is shattered, hit by a big raid late in '44. Many of the buildings that dominated the town in my early years are burnt-out shells. The school still stands. It is scarred by shrapnel, many of the windows are smashed. Even so, our children go there every day and the teachers do the best they can. The little coffee shop that our group used to meet in is just three tables on a patch of pavement that has been cleared of debris. So much destruction, for what?

We escape the ruined town and follow the river, eventually arriving at the place the young Emil Brunnig had fished. The place he had courted and, in time, seduced his first and only love, Helga. So many happy memories, all overshadowed by the memory of the day Max and Heinrich had spied on us. Neither of them will ever return to this spot. So much death, for what?

I am so glad that Helga and the children had been sheltered in the comparative safety of the south. Living in a town taken by the French. Then occupied briefly by the Americans, before being handed back to the care of the French Authorities. Helga hasn't heard the stories about the desperate defence of the capital by old men, women's battalions and children as the Russian tanks smashed their way into the city. The final bloody defeat of the defenders of the city, followed by the rape of Berlin. I am glad that the breakdown in communications across the country has kept Helga in ignorance of the brutality. So much brutality, for what?

Sitting on the banks of the Rhine, dipping our feet in the cold water, I tell Helga of my dream. The one that had scared me so much I couldn't go to Youth Camp, we are already blanking out the name of the former Führer whenever possible, on that Saturday morning.

"You came here to hide from a dream?"

"Yes, it was a frightening dream." I pause mustering all my courage before admitting, "It wasn't just frightening, it was prophetic. I dreamt of the death of Rohm and all his followers, I saw him and his men marching into the hills. Then there was this Jew, a statue, made out of steel. He had been beaten but he was singing. Singing about the eventual defeat of The Reich."

"A dream, you saw this in a dream in 1934?"

"Yes."

"Why didn't you tell anyone?"

"Who? It was a dream!"

"You saw all this destruction and said nothing?"

"I saw this prophesied, not the detail, not the bodies of our friends, our town in ruins. Just the promise that the end would be bad for Germany. Our enemies would grow strong. I remember the words of the statue, 'You can't hold me, I'm strong now, I'm strong. Stronger than your law.' They would have locked me up for being a mad man or a subversive."

"You knew this was coming and you could do nothing to stop it!" Helga's eyes fill with tears.

We lie, holding each other, on the anniversary, wishing my dream of a dozen years ago, about the events of the Night of The

Long Knives, hadn't come true.

The last day of June 1946.

Edward Yeoman

France 1952

Life continues, we struggle on. We are no longer starving. Henri is able to go to school every day, although how much more they are going to be able to teach him I don't know. He corrects his teacher's arithmetic already, despite it only being his sixth birthday. I gather, the teacher told Hélène last night, he took the old classroom clock apart and when he put it back together, it worked. That clock had stopped back in 1942, ten years without a tick or a tock and our son mended it.

Our daughter, Sandrine, has caught up on all the schooling she lost during the war years. She seems to have an ear for languages and has learnt a little English and she speaks Italian, learnt from the PoWs they sent us to help with the harvests. I'm not sure how proper the Italian is, they laugh a lot when she talks to them, the Italian pickers that turn up each summer.

Hélène remains the most beautiful woman I have ever slept with. Mind you, that number has remained unchanged since the day I came back from the war.

Last year we had a good harvest and with a little help from the wine co-operative, I managed to buy a new tractor. Well, not quite new but new to me. It's not what you'd think of as a tractor either. It is an ugly, squat thing on caterpillar tracks that the Americans brought with them for dragging damaged or broken-down tanks across the beach. Old and repurposed it may be but it drags a lot of spray and tools up the hills between the vines and, come the harvest, a big trailer load of grapes to the co-op for crushing.

It proved its strength and power just the other day. We were in M. Duchene's truck, coming back from market laden with cherries for bottling and other tasty treats. Just outside of Perinac we came across a charabanc, it was slewn across the road blocking our path and stuck with both front wheels in the ditch. It was only about a kilometre home, so I set off to fetch the tractor to pull the obstruction out of the way.

I got back to find Sandrine talking to the passengers, while the driver was talking with the Duchenes and Hélène. Henri was studying the charabanc.

I fetched my strong rope out of a storage box and I am about to tie it around the rear axle of the wreck when Henri stops me. "Papa, I think if we get the men back into the rear of the bus and you use the rope to pull the front around a bit first, we might get both of the back wheels on the road again. Then the bus engine could help back the whole thing out of the ditch."

It took a lot of work, me explaining to Sandrine, who explained it to the passengers, who are all Americans. Being Americans, they couldn't believe a small French boy could have the solution to their problem. In the end, Henri had convinced the driver and he had added his nodding and supportive gestures to my imploring. They agreed to try.

It worked, except both front wheels had been buckled and the vehicle was no longer capable of being driven. Henri and the driver took a look underneath and could see no other serious damage. Two new wheels and they could be on their way. The Duchenes took the driver into the village, so that he could phone to Béziers for replacement wheels.

The Americans followed us back to the farm for some refreshments and shade from the summer sun. I chugged along on the tractor, with Hélène bouncing on my knee as the rest walked. Sandrine had found out that they were a group of veterans, revisiting places where friends had fallen in 1944. There was one younger chap with the group, he had joined the veterans to see where his oldest brother had been killed.

Sandrine seemed rather taken with this young man, who she told us later, did speak a little French. He was keen to practice as much as he could. His, what he had called, school, had an exchange with the Sorbonne in Paris and he was determined to get a place.

"Well. if he wants to practice his French, tell him he can come and help us with the harvest," I joke.

In the years to come, I would regret that off the cuff remark. Then that is an unseen future, as we share bread, cheese and wine with a group of our liberators, all sitting under the shade of the walnut trees that surround our house. The trees that I had planted as cuttings back in the autumn of 1941, in the hope of a crop to keep us from starving. Now they have grown tall and bear fruit, but we keep them for the shade they give our garden. Shade in which our guests shelter as they wait for their transport to be repaired and the sun blazes down on us as…

…the last day of June 1952 slips by.

England 1952

The King died in February, we are now New Elizabethans

Hopefully it will herald an era of peace; for the past two years, I have been on readiness for recall to the RAF for Korea. Thankfully the RAF contribution has been small and I have not been called to serve. I have been stood down, I'm now too old for conscription. The new Queen will not command me to send young National Servicemen to their deaths, over a distant country, in outdated aircraft. The Royal Australian Air Force had tried flying the same Gloucester Meteor fighters in combat against the Chinese MIG aircraft and had come off second best.

While our military planes may be dated and outclassed, our new civil jet airliner, the Comet, looks like we are going to continue to be a major force in avionics as we move into the New Elizabethan era.

Meanwhile, Heather and I have paid off the death duties on William's estate. Denham Hall is safe for another generation. I am not sure how the estate would cope in the event of Giles' death but hopefully our seven-year-old will see out several governments before any of them can think about getting their grasping hands on Heather's family home.

We are luckier than many families, some of whom had faced double death duties with both the father dying and then the son in quick succession. We got to hear of estates being given to the nation in their entirety to settle the tax demands. Of desperate widows, wives and mothers trying to negotiate the right to remain in their homes until death. The war has devastated vast areas of the cities, now it is devastating the country set to pay for the rebuilding.

This fate did not befall Denham Hall, it has, however, been tough. A huge number of the works of art collected over the generations by the family have been sold. Many of them at very low prices, so much art has been on the market as the old money families settle their debts to the State.

William's wine cellar has been virtually emptied to enable us to make the final payment to the exchequer.

William had planned for us to sell the collection to a Wine Merchant. I phoned a couple of merchants who were offering to buy up complete cellars of wine. Agents from these merchants came to inspect the collection. They came up with values that both Heather and I were uncomfortable with. They just seemed a bit low, not that we often bought fine wines. We prevaricated about the sale.

It was at a luncheon with one of her Aunts, that Heather had taken the opportunity presented when her Aunt needed to powder her nose. "I'd best do it before we order," her Aunt announced as she slipped away from the table

Heather had taken a careful look at the wine list and seen some names she recognised from our cellar. There was a Château Lafite Rothschild, a 1929 vintage, listed. She was certain that this was one of the wines that the Wine Merchants had been stuffy over.

"I did the sums, Charles," she told me over dinner that evening. "If we have two dozen bottles of that wine it would match the amounts the merchants are offering for the whole cellar!"

"Did you get to try it?" Charles teased gently.

"No chance! Aunt Agatha might have been well-endowed financially by Uncle Bertie, but she doesn't allow alcohol at her table."

"We will have to see if it is exactly the same wine and how much it is selling for in other places."

Next morning, Heather and I carefully noted the details from the labels of the Lafite. Then I made some phone calls to a few hotels and restaurants.

I am, "about to conclude a very lucrative deal with an important client. His favourite wine is Lafite '29." I informed them. "Do you have a bottle, or two, in your cellar? What is it going to cost me?"

The answers amaze me. There are a lot of places that don't have the wine at all and are honest enough to admit it and offer alternatives at several pounds a bottle. A couple of places said yes, they had that wine in stock and matched the price at the restaurant where the ladies had dined yesterday.

One restaurant said bottles would be available for five guineas each. I suspected that if I had made a reservation, they would have been looking to buy some as quickly as possible. The mark-up was considerable.

I am to dine at my old college the following day, "I'll take a closer look at the wine menu than normal." I tell Heather.

It was during that dinner, I discovered just how sought after some of the wines in the Denham Hall cellar were. There were at least a dozen wines that are marked as unavailable or priced over forty shillings a bottle. Our collection houses a gross of some these wines. Nearly three hundred pounds' worth.

"I expect they are making a profit on each bottle though," Heather points out.

"Yes, let's say they sell at twice the price that they pay for any given bottle. The Lafite would still net nearly as much as those spivs were offering for everything." I had heard of friend's elderly relatives, in need of extra cash, being tricked into selling valuable antiques by dealers who paid well under the real value. I hated the idea of us being targeted in with the same type of deception.

We decide to try to sell a couple of cases of wine ourselves. I put the news around a few officers' messes, clubs, friends and university colleges that I have them for sale. The response was pretty much instant; within a week, we could have sold the two cases of White Burgundy three times over.

"It appears that there is a general shortage of good wine available. The Wine Steward at my club is quite concerned," our Accountant informs me, while we are discussing the need to sell some, or all, of the wine to clear the outstanding Death Duty. "People carried on drinking but there was no wine delivery during the war. Then several of London's best wine cellars were destroyed in the bombing and it appears that the military seemed to think they had requisitioned the wine along with the house on more than one estate!"

I explained the response I had received when I had floated the idea to my contacts.

"You've not sold anything yet?" The Accountant became animated. He was worried about the tax situation. The wines had been given a value for probate and the Death Duty. If I sold at above that figure it would have further tax implications. "The chaps that came to value the cellar must have had an idea of the probate figure, that is why they offered pretty much the tax valuation."

"Blast, I was hoping to sell at a higher price and make some money to cover the expenses of this place."

The real value of my trust fund had suffered through poor management over the war years. The value of my shares in the family business was at an all-time low, there was little demand for bayonets, swords and steel-bladed weapons of all types now; with wartime demand for these implements being so high, nothing new had been added to the company's repertoire. The future there looked bleak unless a buyer could be found.

"There is a way …" The Accountant began.

During the next hour, 'Thornton Wines of Denham Co. Ltd' was born. The contents of the cellar at Denham Hall was sold, at exactly the probate valuation figure, to the new company. The two, slightly lower, quotes from other the other merchants would prove that a fair price was paid! The new company was now free to sell the wine at the highest price the market would bear.

"… but we know next to nothing about the price or quality of wines." Heather observed, over our first board room dinner.

"That is very true my sweet and if we want to do this long term, we will need to learn a lot more. However, the Accountant has an idea to get past that. Sealed bid auctions." I continue to explain that we would place advertisements in the Times, every week on a Wednesday.

"Thornton Wines of Denham offer for sale: Two cases of Château de la Reine Pomerol 1932. Two lots of two cases each of Château La Bouche de Loire 1938. Sealed bids to be received for adjudication at 9.00am Monday. Successful bidders will be notified by letter. No post-sale negotiation will be entered into."

"That sounds a very sensible approach for novices like us!"

"That is what I thought too, Heather. If it proves to be enjoyable and profitable, then we set about learning more!"

It was all going well; then I got a phone call from Simon Hurgroves, a former member of my wing at Everoak. "I don't want people to know it is me selling but I have a small number of cases of Beaune 1925 I need to capitalise. I wondered, could you shift a few for me? There would be a commission in it for you, say ten percent for expenses and another ten to make it worthwhile for you?"

I ask a few questions about the provenance and storage of the wine. It appeared that the Hurgroves' family business was going through a bit of a sticky patch. The money was needed to tide it through some serious financial talks, without causing a loss of confidence. I agree to give it a go, subject to a tasting. I wasn't going to risk our nascent reputation as suppliers of quality wine.

A phone call to my old college resulted in me driving a retired sommelier north to the Hurgroves' place and my first lesson in the finer points of wine tasting. It was fascinating trying to pick out the hints in the mix of flavours that told Mr Rogers that this wine was just passing its peak. He advised me that, as long as I advertised that this vintage was for immediate drinking, it would not only sell well but having it in the company's portfolio for a while would enhance our reputation.

The business actually thrived. We were soon selling wines for a lot of our set and their friends. All looked good until somebody joked about being able to afford to buy some 1947 Bordeaux after we got them an exceptionally good price on some Mouton-Cadet.

New wines, that would reduce the demand for the remaining pre-war stock. It was time for me to venture into the world of wine. Mr Rogers had helped me develop a palate and given me a grounding in the great wine-producing regions of France, Germany and Italy. It was on his advice that I decided to specialise in French wines and those of Bordeaux and the Loire in particular.

Favours were called in, promises made and I was off to South Western France. I recalled talking with with Heather as I packed "I wonder if that French pilot, who gave me lift made it?" and "I hope they managed to fix up 'Lewy', Louis, as I'm sure his name was". Within days, I was grateful for the promise I had made after those encounters back in 1940 as I focussed my concentration on the conversation between my guide and a less than famous wine producer

My guide, who had fought at Verdun in 1917, was a friend of a friend of Mr Rogers. He had arranged appointments with many of the

Grand Vintners and at some of the famous châteaux of the region. He had also taken it upon himself to take me to taste some of the famous wines of the region.

    As he explained it, the big names dealt with the big names amongst the British wine importers. I might be able to pick up some scraps at their table. On the other hand, there were several growers and producers who had come on in leaps and bounds due to the demands of the German occupiers. They were looking for new markets, I was looking for new suppliers. Monsieur Charreau had finally understood the concept that I was looking to buy more than a couple of cases of wine to take home.

    We went for a walk around his carefully tended vines, where the tiny fruit were just starting to develop. Then into his cave lined with huge barrels and concrete cuvées. This was a huge learning curve, I realised, and I was still near the bottom. Then he pulled the corks on several bottles: last year's bottling, a five-year-old and an eight-year-old bottle. He wiped a couple of glasses and we tasted.

    The youngest was heavy with tannin that sucked the inside of my mouth dry. My guide explained the hints that made him think this was going to be a good wine. The five-year-old was nice, I'd have been happy to drink it with a good steak and kidney at my club.

Then there was the oldest bottle, the German Weinführer had bought all the previous bottlings, this was an absolute delight. All the notes Mr Rogers had taught me to look for were there. The balance was good and my guide assured me that this wine would keep for another few years if treated carefully.

"May I taste the two missing years?" M. Charreau appeared to have got the hang of my accent. The bottles immediately appear on the tasting table, their corks removed allowing them a short respite to breathe.

A week later, I'm back at Château Charreau. We have agreed on a price for one hundred cases of the eight-year-old with special labelling,

"Thornton's of Denham,

Château bottled Bordeaux

by Château Charreau"

There are another hundred cases with M.Charreau's normal label in reserve. In addition, I have secured options on both custom-labelled and unlabelled bottles of the next four years' vintages. If they sell as well as I think they will, the investment will pay off.

Edward Yeoman

I hope that the last day of June 1952
turns out to be as an auspicious date as it feels
it should be as I sign our contract, in twenty-six
places, while a *Notaire* watches us both.

Germany 1952

"Emil, I understand that your French is pretty good?" The Head of Strategic Planning has just entered the Rural Planning Office.

"I have some skill," I reply as a massive wave of déjà vu sweeps over me.

"Good, I have a little job for you …"

That was 1950, as I recall. Things were on the up for the people of Germany and, more importantly, the Brunnig family. After the war, we had endured the Hungerwinter of 1947. The intense cold and the lack of coal for heating. The lack of food, near-starvation rations and an exhausted and empty black market.

We had lost three people in our household alone; Herr Lang had gone out to try to find some coal and frozen to death while queuing overnight outside a depot rumoured to be getting a delivery. My mother had developed bronchitis and died of cold when we had opened the windows. It was a better death than gasping for breath as she drowned from within; Frau Bergmann had starved herself to death, feeding her grandchildren a little extra and herself not at all. Herr Bergmann had taken the two grandchildren and headed to his sister's house near Leipzig. With the birth of the German Democratic Republic, we had lost contact with them.

I was released by the French Military Authorities during the following winter and I had secured a job in the Planning Department. The economy had started to expand noticeably and by 1950, things were starting to look good. There was a good chance that our teenage children would have a better life than we had endured.

Then serendipity, in the form of a suspicious Director of Planning, had taken me by the hand and guided me to a better place, again.

The French wanted to build a new Autoroute, Autobahn this side of the border. The Boss, quite rightly, had the impression we were about to be stitched up. The Official Translator in the meetings was a Frenchman. The German Translator provided by the State didn't have the technical language and everyone had the feeling that something was being lost, probably deliberately hidden, in the translation.

I was inserted into the negotiating team as a Rural Planning expert and undercover translator. Just as well really. The translator provided by the French was doing an honest job of translating words, just he was less open on the hidden, idiomatic language. However, that wasn't all the French were up to.

The line on the map took the new road on an interesting curve through the countryside. "Straight roads are dangerous, too hypnotic, too easy to speed, too easy to fall asleep." That bit of translation was pretty accurate. Then there was the Rest Area with full services, that needed access roads, "To get the workers in from the surrounding area."

All very good except, the proposed route carved right across some of the best vineyards of Baden with even more productive land being ploughed up for the Rest Area and the support infrastructure. I was probably the only person in the State of Baden with the knowledge to pick this up.

How many experienced French to German translators, with an insider's knowledge of the ruthless French wine trade and understanding of planning were there in Southern Germany?

So now, two years later, I work in the big new office building in Strasbourg. I have become a bureaucrat, looking after matters of the grape and wine for the Council of Europe.

Who was better qualified for the role? I spoke German and French; I was rapidly acquiring a little Italian and a smattering of Spanish. When I stop confusing the words in the two Latin languages, I would be better. Still, French was the most important language in wine.

I had learnt about wine and the wine trade under the auspices of the Bordeaux Weinführer; who I have discovered, is still active in the business. I sometimes pick up little bits of tittle-tattle from my ex-Kommandant. Then, I know where one or two of the metaphorical bodies remained buried. Even if I have decided to keep that information to myself, I could, and he, and several others, don't know I won't, lead men with spades to good places to dig the dirt.

Later this summer, I have several meetings to attend. I am planning to take the family with me, then we will travel on for our family holiday. I gather that the Spanish Mediterranean coast offers several beautiful beachside resorts. I have been reliably informed that, unlike much of the rest of Europe, the people of Spain hold no animosity to Germans. Strange, that in defeat, I can offer my family something that wasn't possible at the height of the Reich, a holiday at the beach. That is the state of the world on the last day of June 1952.

France 1960

In October 1954, our daughter, Sandrine, went on a trip to Paris to help her pen-friend Tommy settle into his apartment. The two of them had kept up a steady exchange of letters since the autumn Tommy came to help us with the harvest.

Don't get me wrong, Tommy, Thomas J Albright Jnr, was a pleasant, young man. His family was also pretty well to do and he is the eldest surviving son of the 'Chemicals' Family. That doesn't mean a lot to me, but I am told, in the United States, there are a group of families who became rich from being in at the start of various industries, steel, railways,oil and chemicals for example.

It was just that Hélène and I knew we were losing our little girl. The evidence was clear to see. Since Tommy had arrived in August 1952, Sandrine had not paid the slightest attention to any of the local boys who tried to court her. We were just disappointed that she was not honest with us. Even when she returned home two weeks' later.

"Papa, Maman! I am going back to Paris to study English." The 'and be with Tommy' hung silent in the air. "I have a place at The Institute of Business Language."

The young woman that came home for a few days over Christmas that year was a different Sandrine. She was still our loving daughter but her hair was coiffured and coloured. The clothes she wore were new, fitted, stylish and, with rationing still in place, expensive. She stayed for nearly two weeks, sleeping in her old bed. Helping her mother in the kitchen. Playing with her little brother.

Even at the age of eight, Henri had outgrown the village school and was getting into trouble. He was more interested in machines and making things than schoolwork. He was a great help around the farm, inventing things that made life that little easier for an effectively one-armed man.

I had never regained any use in my damaged left hand. Henri had fitted a spike to the steering wheel of the tractor. My wrecked hand fitted over the spike and I could steer left-handed, allowing me to use my right to hold and carry.

One evening, just before Sandrine was to return to Paris, I found my two children deep in conversation. Before I could speak, Sandrine gestured me away, I returned to the kitchen.

"I don't know what they are talking about," I said to Hélène, as she stirred the potage for our supper. "Sandrine didn't want me to interfere. So, I left her to it."

"She has grown up a lot, that young lady. You know she will be asking to get married next summer?" Hélène pushed her hair back behind her ear. I notice that there are more strands of grey than there had been during the summer.

"Next summer?"

"Tommy's year at the Sorbonne finishes. If she is going to America, she will have to be his wife."

"Do you think we can raise a big enough dowry?" We were getting by but we still were on the edge, a bad harvest, the loss of our chickens, we were in trouble.

"I gather that rich, American families don't pay or expect dowries. They do, however, encourage marriages to consolidate wealth."

"Oh."

Sandrine had silently slipped into the kitchen behind me.

"Mamma, Papa, please. If Tommy wants to marry me, he will. We have talked about it. He says he is in a strong position as the only son of the family. They can't disinherit him." She paused. "I have been talking to Henri, I think he now understands that if he wants to become an engineer, he has to get good marks at school. He has promised me he will work hard in all subjects. That way when he applies to go to university, maybe in Paris. He will have glowing reports and references."

This was the first I had heard of Henri and engineering.

"Thank you, Sandrine, I have been so worried about Henri losing interest at school, it would be such a waste." Hélène knew more than I did, naturally.

*****

I wasn't able to go to Sandrine's wedding. Hélène and Henri made the long trip north to Paris. I had to stay and care for the farm animals. I was happy that Hélène had a chance to see the sights of the capital. I had spent a few days there during those heady few weeks before we lost the Battle of France. In the days when I was young, I had two good strong hands and old Henri was still alive. I was touched that Sandrine had chosen to marry on the 30th June.

She had sent me a little note. "Papa, I had hoped you could come to the wedding, I understand that it is not possible. I have decided on the date because it is the most important day in the year for me. The day when you became my Papa, twice over. The day I met Tommy and now the day I will marry him. Think of me at 11 o'clock on the 30th June. Your loving daughter, Sandrine"

I still have that note, tucked carefully inside the family Bible.

The Last Day of June

*****

Sandrine moved to America with her new husband. She writes to her mother every month. Last year, Tommy was on some trade mission to the new European Economic Community. Sandrine came with him, along with my grandsons. During a week of trade talks, whatever they are, she came to stay with us for a couple of days. Hélène was like an old mother hen, clucking around her chicks.

Even Henri emerged from his books to be with his sister and nephews.

"I'm so glad you listened to me Henri. How is it all going?" Sandrine asked over the evening meal.

"It is going well. I struggle a bit with Latin and history, but I am getting good passes."

I didn't know Henri was learning Latin. I began to suspect that any hopes I had of Henri taking over the farm were false.

"Any news from Toulouse?"

What was going on? I am lost, Toulouse?

"I got a letter, they will accept me a year early, if I keep my marks up."

"And you are doing that, aren't you Henri?" Hélène smiled proudly.

My wife knew what was going on, so all was good. I'll ask her later.

Sandrine's stay is too short but she had to get back to Paris. There was a formal dinner. She and Tommy were going to be guests of the President of France, General de Gaulle.

This was a day I would remember for a long time. Kicking a ball around with my grandchildren. My daughter about to meet the President of the Republic. My son has a place to study Aeronautical Engineering at Toulouse, as long as he keeps his nose in his books and clean from trouble.

The European Economic Community might have generated a pile of forms to fill in. I am blessed to have Henri to help explain them to me. My clever son understands them and shows me what to put in each box. The reward has been better prices for our wine and olive oil. At last, we can afford a little comfort.

My wonderful wife and I will drive Sandrine and the boys to the station in Montpellier in our family car.

The date? Of course it's the 30th June 1960!

England 1960

The Fifties hadn't been a very good decade for the British. Korea and Suez had damaged national self-confidence. There is a marked anti-military sentiment; so much so that the Campaign for Nuclear Disarmament attracts huge numbers of marchers and the papers reported that almost one hundred thousand people were at a big Ban the Bomb demonstration in London earlier this year.

We, the Thornton family, had done all right, despite the doom and gloom, there are now four of us. Giles has a sister, Sophie. The business is doing well, even though the buying and selling of pre-war wine collections has more or less dried up. On my trips to France, I have found several more makers of wines that people seem to like. I have also noticed that year by year, we are bringing in more and more wine. It seems the British thirst is on the increase, despite, or maybe because of, the tough times we have been going through.

There are also signs that the post-war depression is starting to lift. The youngsters are dancing to a different kind of music. Heather and I went to a party the other week, where we danced to some of the tunes we used to dance to before the war. Mind you, it was a case of dancing to records, rather than a proper band. Then, as we began to tire, the youngsters started to play some of those American 'rocking roll' records. It all sounded very energetic and exciting.

Mind you, we are well versed in the latest music. Giles bombards us with records by Cliff Richard, who is some sort of English Elvis Presley, and Lonnie Donegan. For his birthday last winter, Giles, who is now fourteen, demanded an electric guitar. He is part of a fledgling skiffle group at school.

We bought him an acoustic instrument and promised him an electric set up for his Christmas and birthday presents, providing he is making progress with the acoustic. I think we have made a rod for our own backs. At Easter, he spent hours in his room practising. We even had to endure a couple of boys coming to stay for group rehearsals.

It must have made some sort of difference, we got a letter from Giles to say that the group, The Five Anchorians, would be performing at the end of term concert. Heather is suddenly worried about going this year. I suppose it is one thing for your son to be in the choir, as Giles had been. It is rather different to have him doing his first-ever performance of skiffle at the school as his first solo flight. Yes, there are five of them but they will no longer be under the supervision of a teacher.

I'd have hated to have my parents watching the first time I took off for a solo flight at Cranwell. In fact, if memory serves, I didn't tell them I had gone solo for a week. The only person not part of my course, who knew, was Heather.

The same Heather who is fussing around, panicking about her son's concert in two weeks' time. Should we take the girls? Who can we get to look after them? Should she get a new dress?

I said, "Yes, of course." Which then changed to, what sort of dress is suitable for one of the stars of the concert? Is it appropriate to dress as the mother of a star of the concert? Is being in a skiffle group being a star of the concert? What about being part of the first public performance of skiffle in the school's history? Did that make him a star?

I decide that was too much of a specialist subject for man. "Why don't you ring Audrey? I'm sure she will be able to advise you!"

"Oh, Charles, you are such a wise man at times!" Heather picks up the phone. At the same time, I pick up the car keys. "Where are you going?" The phone must be still ringing at the other end.

"Shopping," I reply.

"Hello, Audrey, just a second, I need a word with Charles." She puts her hand over the mouthpiece. "Shopping?"

"Yes, I'm going to get myself a pair of blue suede shoes and a leather jacket!" I announce and duck out of the door.

"Charles! Charles!" She calls after me.

"See you later alligator!" I call out and shut the door behind me.

It is the last day of June 1960 and I am such a 'cool daddio' as the hipsters say on the radio.

Germany 1960

In 1958 I was recruited into the new European Economic Community bureaucracy. I am to be part of the Agricultural Policy Planning Team for the Common Market that had just been created.

Two years' later, all my skills are in play again, languages, knowledge of wine, working across national borders. I have become a leading German member of the wine team, a functionary. A very important functionary, a very well-paid functionary. I travel across Europe, talking to local producer groups about the new European regulations. The new intervention buying that is supposed to help keep the market stable. I listen to their feedback and pass it up the line, I advise the Commissioner and he advises the Council of Ministers, who then adjust the policy.

My colleagues then take the new policy and turn it into rules and regulations that the Commission and the Council of Ministers approve. Then, next year, I will go out and explain the new rules and regulations to the farmers and so the cycle will continue until everyone is getting a fair reward for their work. It is not Communism mind you, if you only make a basic wine you will only get a basic price. Produce a better wine and you get to keep all the money, except for the tax of course.

It will take years to get it right, until then I am empowered to travel around Southern Europe and take my wife with me. I can even take my holiday entitlement before or just after one of these trips. This year I think we might be in Provence during July.

It will be the first time we will have holidayed without our children, Dieter stopped coming with us a couple of years ago. Now, with his new job working for BMW and a new girlfriend in Munich, we don't see him that often. Antje, our daughter is away at university studying to become a lawyer and will have to take a summer job at an *Anwaltskanzlei*, an intern, to gain practical experience of life in a solicitor's office this year.

I have had a day off work today, a trip to the Doctor's for a routine medical revealing that I am in good shape. I was given the all-clear just after lunch; I am sitting in the shade of a typical French café in this city with a German name, that is home to a pan-European organisation. While I am waiting for my wife to join me, I drink coffee watching the waters of the Rhine slip past on its long journey to the North Sea.

Maybe I drift off to sleep; I am looking at a young man, on the other bank, sitting alone, trailing his feet in the water. A giggle causes me to look a bit further back from the water, a couple are making love, when the man jumps to his feet and … "Emil! there you are!" Helga's voice calls me back to the café, back to 1960 and the realisation that it is the last day of June.

Edward Yeoman

France 1967

1966 had been a mixed year for the Verdier family. The farm had been profitable, we had got a good price for our grapes from the Co-op. I heard that a wine merchant in Bordeaux had bought a couple of tankers of our wine a week. I didn't ask what he was doing with it. Sometimes it is best not to know too much about the dealings of your customers.

Henri has done well in his studies, completed his Licence and was accepted for a master's degree course. We were so proud, a farmer and his wife, to watch him receive his diploma.

The news from the United States was not so good. Sandrine and Tommy's marriage was in trouble. Eventually, it turned into a divorce. Tommy might not have been as generous as he might have been financially, but he has allowed the grandchildren to return to France with their mother. They will have to spend each August in America with the family in the Hamptons. Which, as Sandrine said, was about as much as they got to see him before.

Hélène and I were both delighted to spend Christmas in Paris with our grandchildren. We were even happier to hear that Sandrine would be moving back to Perinac in the late spring. We gather that she is enrolled to complete one of the courses that got interrupted when she departed to America.

We had a party to welcome them all to the village, which we combined with my fifty-fifth birthday. All the village turned out and we ate, drank and danced late into the night. Our two very American young men wandered around looking completely bemused. I don't think they have parties like this where they lived.

The next day we sat down as a family and discussed the future. The conversation didn't go the way I expected. Nor for that matter, Hélène. We were thinking in terms of adding a couple of bedrooms and an indoor bathroom with a water closet, or two, to the house. Then we would live together as a family, the way our parents' generation had before the wars.

"You do realise that Henri has no interest in taking on the farm, don't you?"

We both nodded, over the years we had come to recognise that Henri had no interest in the farm that had once belonged to his namesake. What Sandrine said next though was a complete surprise.

"Well, I want it, I want to run it, I want to run it my way starting from the end of the harvest this year." Sandrine stopped and left us to absorb this stunning statement.

"I don't understand why Sandrine? I thought Tommy had given you enough to live on. Why do you want to slave on this farm for a pittance?" Hélène asked the question that I was still trying to put into words.

"It is not the money and I have no intention of slaving for a pittance any more than you are now!" She looked us both in the eye before continuing. "There are very rich men in the wine trade. Men who don't slave in the fields but have huge amounts of money from the wines they make. Men in Bordeaux, men in the *Rhône* Valley and now there are men in California getting rich from wine. Why can't I get rich too, growing wine on my family's land?"

"They make better wine than our Co-op. That way they get a better price." Hélène repeated the traditional wisdom of the Languedoc.

"Why? Do they make a wine worth ten times what ours is? No. They make a wine that people want to buy and are prepared to pay more for. They spent years choosing the right grapes, grown on the right terroir and learning to balance the flavour. We, I mean the people of this region, grow as many grapes as possible and sell them by the tonne to the local Co-op, who make vinegar!"

"Not completely true!" I butt in. "Our Co-op now sells a lot of wine to people in Bordeaux." That took the wind out of Sandrine's sails for a few seconds.

"You know what that means, don't you? It means they are blending it into wines being sold at premium prices. It proves the Languedoc can produce good wine."

"But we can only get what the Co-op will pay us, no matter how good our grapes!" Hélène, a daughter of the region, was having difficulty seeing beyond the valley that contains Perinac and all of her life.

"You want us to make our own wine and sell it ourselves don't you, Sandrine?" I had worked in other areas, I had pruned and picked for *châteaux* that made their own wines in the days of my youth. I know it can be done. "It will take a lot of money for equipment, money that we haven't got. It will take new varieties of vines that will take time to become established."

"I know this, I have the money promised to me for the vats, pumps and barrels we will need to buy. The bottling and labelling I will find the money for. Meanwhile, I have a five-year plan. I will go to college and learn about the arts of the vigneron. We will replant the vineyard and we will continue to sell to the Co-op. Then we will start to make some of our own wine from some of our grapes, if it works, we will make more, until one day, Domaine Verdier will be a wine people pay a premium price for."

"A dream, daughter!"

"No, Hélène, hear her out. What is the plan for this year if we agree to your idea?"

"I will be going to college to learn about making good quality wine. We harvest as normal and sell to the Co-op. Then we clear a few rows of the older Carignan vines and put in some Grenache to reduce the tannin in our wine. Meanwhile, I will bring in the builders to put up a new house for me and the children with a built-in cave to make life in the future easier."

"That sounds like a good first step, although your mother and I were going to have an extension put on the old house for you."

"I appreciate that and while I need to work with you in the vines, Papa, learning as much of the ways that have sustained this farm as possible. I do not think two women can work in one kitchen, especially as the children prefer to eat the meatloaf they know over the cassoulet of this region. What say you Mama, do you want me in your kitchen? Making foreign dishes? Using a gas oven?"

"Maybe not, but the wine revolution?

That I need time to decide on."

"We will talk between ourselves, the four of us, Henri has a say too. Then Mama and I will make a decision. So that this doesn't drag on forever, we will tell you on the Family Day."

That is today. Henri's birthday, he has taken a few days off from his studies, claiming a family crisis that requires his attention to escape from Toulouse. The four of us assemble around the kitchen table. The grandchildren have been sent to school, with the promise that Uncle Henri will build a windmill for them tomorrow, if they are good.

"Henri, as our son and the presumptive heir to this farm, you will be the first to speak. Do you want to take over the running of the farm, now or in the future?"

"Papa, I know you have to ask, but no. I have no interest in the farm, if my sister Sandrine wishes to run it, I will resign my birthright to her."

"Sandrine, you are the instigator of this family conversation about the future of the farm, do you have any new, last-minute thoughts on the subject?"

"No Papa."

"Hélène, it was through your inheritance

that this farm came to the family. Do you have any last comments?"

"No, I just ask Sandrine to heed your advice and not to ignore tradition without good reason."

"Mama, I will depend on Papa until my dying day and I realise that traditions survive because they worked. I will build new traditions, on Papa's experience, on the wisdom of ages, that will meet the needs of the future."

"Then, my daughter, it is time for the builders to start work on turning this farm into the Domaine …"

"Verdier, Papa, the Domaine Verdier, without you none of us would be here having this conversation. I will always remember you struggling to carry the last basket of grapes to the cart each evening, the Domaine Verdier will only exist because of your blood sweat and tears."

That was two hours ago; since then I have shed more tears into the soil of the Domaine Verdier. Tears of love, joy and pride for my family on the most special day in our family calendar… June 30th 1967, a date that I will carry in my heart forever.

Edward Yeoman

England 1967

The Post World Cup euphoria of last summer is just a memory of a time passed. The Government appears to be in turmoil, there was a threat of the pound being devalued, although that is being talked down. A devaluation would not be desperately good for the wine business; it would put all the prices up and demand would go down. I suppose that is the idea, the balance of payments, well let's just agree, it is not the best of news.

"Do you think that we will still be on the wine list at Ascot next year?" Heather had asked, as she put her hat back into its box after last week's extravaganza of horse racing.

"Nearly all the people I spoke to thought our wines were very good, especially at their price." It was part of a conversation that had been going on since the start of the financial year.

Until this year, things had been going so well. I bought new wines on my trips to France and Spain. They were shipped in huge crates back to my warehouse, in Harwich, where we store them in the cool and dark until they are shipped to our customers across the length and breadth of Great Britain. Heather and I have been spending hours with our sales agents, trying to get to grips with the mood in the market. Should we be bold and bullish, increasing our purchasing along with historic trends? Or, would it be better to be a little circumspect; buy a little less and use pricing to restrict or stimulate demand?

After a lot of soul-searching and debate, for the first time in this business, I decide to err on the side of caution. I have been signing letters to some of our suppliers declining options to purchase, this year only. I make sure that the letter expresses our confidence in a return to growth next year.

"I desperately wanted to wait until after next Wednesday to send these letters, however, tomorrow is the date in the contracts." I look up from this thankless task.

"I know, but if it all goes well at Henley next week, I am sure you could place the orders again, maybe at a slightly higher price but I agree, we do need to be cautious this coming year." It was good to hear my wife and business partner is still on the same page as me.

We had decided to take a marquee at The Royal Regatta, one of my former colleagues was on the team charged with making the dry-side activities more profitable. As a favour to him I had booked a pitch, at the time as a tax loss, but now…

"I'm sure we will secure new customers, maybe even some of the caterers will take our wines on!" Heather must have been reading my mind.

I place the cap back on my pen and return it to my pocket. The secretary would pick up the signed letters and see they were dispatched.

"Are you ready to leave now, dear?"

I scan my desk, check the clock, half-past-three on a Friday. "I don't expect anything that can't wait until Monday. So, yes, let's make tracks."

As we head out through the doors, I call out to Gail, our secretary, "We are off to London now. I have left the post on my desk. If anybody phones, tell them I will call them back on Monday."

"Right-ho, Mr Thornton, Mrs Thornton. Have a good weekend and enjoy the concert!"

"Thank you, Gail. I hope your weekend goes well too!" I shut the door of the building and hurry down the steps to the Jaguar, where I open the car door for Heather. A few minutes later we are on the road towards London and supper at the Royal Air Force Club.

Tomorrow, Giles is playing in a free

concert in Trafalgar Square. The Five Anchorians left school, replaced a few members of the line-up and "The Book of Malachi" was born. They have been on Top of the Pops a couple of times. Heather had a party the first time, about twenty couples for dinner. I had rented several TVs from Radio Rentals for the week.

In general, "The Book of Malachi" eschew the pop scene. Giles explained to his aged parents that that future lies in album sales. I expect he's right.

He is now a sitting Member of the House of Lords. It was just a couple of months ago that he made his maiden speech in the Chamber. He spoke in opposition to the Marine Broadcasting Offences Bill, during a debate in May. I must say that his Lordships paid a lot of attention to what he said. Giles is still the youngest member of the House and, as an active musician, was considered an expert in the field.

Since Easter 1964 a number of commercial radio stations playing non-stop popular music had appeared along the coast of Britain. These new, so called radio pirates were unregulated. Many of the people involved were at best chancers. The Government was seeking the powers to regain control of airwaves. Much to the chagrin of young people and parts of the popular music industry. The

Marine Offences bill was the governments choice of weapon.

He spoke against the Bill in the other readings and forced a few amendments to the Bill. Arguing that some form of licensing and gentle regulation would be sufficient. The pirates were self-funding through advertisements. They gave a popular outlet for young people to express their individuality and were a shop window for British popular music. An industry that is major source of export earnings and tax revenue.

Sadly, I heard on the evening news, all his efforts have been in vain. The House of Commons considered and rejected all the amendments to the Bill proposed by the House of Lords.

Tomorrow, July first's protest demonstration will be to no avail. I expect Pirate Radio will be gone within a few weeks. I am not sure that banning young people from enjoying something as harmless as listening to what they want to on the radio is why so many of my friends gave their lives…

The last day of June 1967

Edward Yeoman

Germany 1967

It has only been weeks since June 2nd. During protests about a visit from the Shah of Iran, a West Berlin Police Officer shot and killed leftist demonstrator Benno Ohnesorg. His killing has spooked Helga; Ohnesorg was 26, the same age as Kurt, our daughter Antje's husband. He too is a bit of a political rebel, with strong social views. Thankfully, he is close to us in Strasbourg and wasn't in Berlin on that day. I gather from what is now starting to appear in the newspapers, that things got rather brutal, with the police using violence as a first resort. Have they not learnt anything from the 30s?

Kurt has told me that many students and people with socialist ideas are very angry about the killing. They are even angrier about the cover-up in the press and the signs of a whitewash of the police actions, including the shooting. He has apparently stopped going to some meetings, there is so much anger. Some radicals are talking about revenge and revolution. There are many very angry young people.

I'll admit that I am less than happy with the lack of change that has taken place since we regained our independence from the occupying powers. It is as if we are stuck in a time where everything in our lives is controlled by the military. Like many of my generation, my youth was controlled by the Government. We had activities that we were expected to join in. Other activities that were frowned upon, some to a point where you disappeared. We had our lives laid out for us, service to the Fatherland, even motherhood was a patriotic duty. Then we died, in our hundreds of thousands, in the service of the Führer.

I have a different vision for the remainder of our lives. It comes, directly, from our former occupiers, The Americans, their continual optimism, despite the murder of their President, Mr Kennedy. The dream of freedom and individual happiness conveyed in so many of their movies. The British, with the crazy fashions, wild music and eccentric art also make me think that there must be another way.

Then I suppose Helga and I have a clearer picture of what life could be like than others. Our travels take us all over southern Europe, so we see life in Italy and France. We have taken holidays in the dictatorship that is Spain and have seen changes there too.

Even the French, it seems, have taken up the idea of individual freedom. Last summer, Helga and I were in Provence for a month where we found many women were sun-bathing with their breasts uncovered. Which, I have since discovered, used to be common in Germany before the rise of the

Nazis when such things were banned. We are planning to take our holiday in the same region again this summer. I hope that the relaxed attitude to clothing has continued. I spent too many years in uniform and since then in a business suit, I feel a little rebellion of my own coming on.

I am beginning to feel that if I don't do something soon it will be too late. Then I suppose my sense of mortality is up. I heard the news on the radio about Jane Mansfield being killed in a car crash before I came into work. Young, rich, famous and free one minute, dead the next. It made me think of Max and Heinrich, both dead these twenty-odd years, I wonder if either of them got to sit in the sunshine watching the waves lapping on a sandy shore? What a waste, it must never happen again.

Just a few weeks, while the kerfuffle at work, caused by Britain formally applying to become a member of the Common Market, dies down. That should enable us to get away mid-July as usual.

Edward Yeoman

France 1974 - Morning

"Merde! How can I have done that?"

"What is it Sandrine? Can I help?" So, even my daughter fouls up sometimes, although I expect it is a case of putting her grey blouse in the wash with her whites or something major like that.

There are just the two of us, we are looking through the paperwork concerning the wines we are making. Something we do together every Sunday after breakfast, sitting in the shade away from the late morning heat. Sandrine is in the house on the phone to our son wishing him a very happy birthday. His job with Aérospatiale had kept him, his wife and our granddaughter in Toulouse, then that is his life choice.

"It's Sunday! Why is the man from the EEC coming to see us on a Sunday? I thought he meant next year! That is why I booked the Englishman and his wife for today. He is important, his company has a reputation for bringing unknown wines to the British market."

"Is that why you have Mama slaving away in the kitchen preparing a banquet? There was I thinking you were hoping to get some tourist to take six bottles rather than two!"

"Papa, this is serious!"

"I know, but every time something appears to have gone wrong at this farm, it has worked out well. I will tell Mama to set places for three guests."

"Four, the man from the Common Market is bringing his wife too."

That actually sounds like good news to me. In my, albeit limited experience, when a government official has his wife with him, it is a harmless visit. I'll not pass on this bit of wisdom to Sandrine; in case I am wrong.

*****

I am up in the vines; it is hot, then it nearly always is at this time of year. The fruit has set and there are no signs of any of the hundred and one things that can infest the grapes. When I hear the noise of a car changing gear, looking down the slope I see a white Mercedes moving slowly towards the house; the German from the Common Market, I presume.

I'd better get back down to the farm and make sure the cave is looking business-like, ready for the tastings. According to Sandrine's plan, she will do the presentation as the professional, forward-facing, multi-lingual face of La Domaine Verdier.

I am supposed to represent the history of the farm, the terroir, the traditions of wine cultivation and production that runs back to the Romans. Which is fine by me, because that is what I am and my skills as the opener of bottles and the serving of food and wine are restricted. What is that old joke about a one-armed waiter?

Hélène is, of course, the glamourous hostess, mistress of the country kitchen. The wonder woman who will magic up the delightful fare that will appear effortlessly at the huge scrubbed table under the walnut trees. Except, that these dishes were researched and have been prepared half a dozen times to perfect the balance of flavours to bring out the best in the wine that Sandrine has been making in increasing quantities for the past four years.

The boys have been packed off on their bikes with a picnic and instructions not to return until three o'clock. I don't think that this will be too much of a chore, the picnic was very generous. More than enough for four, should someone, say a couple of *mademoiselles* from their school, choose to join them. I am not that old that I have forgotten what happened under the olive trees all those summers ago.

This was a routine we had developed over the winter months. It had been tested a few weeks earlier when we had invited a group of Dutch wine buffs to a tasting. We had done the full show for them and sold a dozen cases of wine, not quite enough to cover costs but very close. Today, we have planned to repeat the event for someone with far more purchasing power.

The European Bureaucrat could be a problem or just maybe a deal maker.

As I reach the safety of the cave, I see Sandrine greeting the grey-haired man and his slightly rotund wife. Everything about them shouts "German." The car, his haircut and bearing. Her shape and slightly reticent behaviour. They are Germans.

As I am taking this in, a silver-grey Jaguar pulls up alongside the Mercedes. Only the British build and drive cars like that. It has to be the anticipated buyer, Mr Thornton, with his wife. It was strange, that apart from my daughter, all of us have to be in our sixties.

I went back to checking the barrels in which last year's vintage was maturing. That was the story anyway. The truth be told, I am splashing a little of it around, just enough to give a hint of wine aroma to the spotlessly clean winery.

"This is my father and the inspiration behind La Domaine Verdier, Louis Verdier." Sandrine had brought the buyer and the man from the Common Market in to see where the wine is made and to have a tasting. The bottles and glasses are laid out waiting, along with water and a spittoon.

"Papa, come and meet Mr and Mrs Thornton, from England."

"Charles and Heather, please! Bonjour M. Verdier." I shake hands with the English couple.

"And this is Herr und Frau Brunnig, from Germany, via the CEE."

"Emil and Helga, please M. Verdier. We are pleased to make your acquaintance." The German spoke French almost as well as I do and far better than my few words of occupation German or the little English I had learnt from the boys. Then this was Sandrine's show.

She takes them around the cave, talking about the processes and ...suddenly she stops. "But you know all this! Let us taste the wines by themselves before we try them as an accompaniment to Mama's wonderful food. She leads the party to the tasting table. I watch as the English get deeply involved in the tasting. The Germans less so, it appears they want to talk to Sandrine. I move closer to listen in; they are talking French.

"Well, the EEC, sorry CEE policy of buying all the wine produced at a fixed price is, in my opinion, starting to distort the market. It is unsustainable, in a few years we will be swimming in a lake of cheap, almost undrinkable wine. I think what you are doing here may be the way forwards. At the moment this is still a private thought, I am not here in any official capacity, yet! Hence making our visit here on the first Sunday of my holiday."

"That sounds very interesting, Emil, I'd like to hear what you have to say, being in the business." The Englishman's French was not as good as the German's but it was the best I had ever heard an Englishman speak my language.

"If Madam Sandrine doesn't mind. I think your contribution would be useful."

"And I would be more than happy to espouse my views to all and sundry, Herr Brunnig, Emil. Let's carry on the discussion around the table."

My daughter, 'espousing' to the man from the CEE. I am so proud of her.

France 1974 - Lunchtime

Our Hostess, Sandrine, it's not Verdier but I can't recall how she signed the letters just now, escorted Heather and Helga across the courtyard towards a table arranged in the shade of some trees. Emil tagged on just behind them. I am hanging back to speak to M. Verdier.

"This is an impressive enterprise you and your family are building, M Verdier." My, I am getting bad at names, or maybe I hadn't been told his first name. "Has the farm been in your family for a long time?"

"Yes, and no. It came to my wife when her first husband was killed."

"In the war?"

"Yes, he was in the infantry and was killed in the battle of Arras in 1940."

"Yes, a lot of good men died during those early weeks of the war. I hope we never have to send our grandsons off to war like that."

"Absolutely, M. Thornton, absolutely!"

As we walk on, I notice M. Verdier's lace has come undone. I point it out and wait while he re-ties it, almost one-handed. I notice that his left hand is frozen.

He straightens up and hurries me to the table. "Quick, before my lovely wife Hélène, loses patience with me and I end up wearing the entrée. That would be such a waste!"

The older women seem to have congregated around one end of the table. They appear to be taking delight in finding commonalities between them. They all have names that start with Aitch, Hah or Hash depending on which of them are talking. Which surprises me, I thought that Mme Verdier was called 'Ellen' but I discover she is Hélène.

I start to feel slightly sorry, Mme Albright, the name returned to me in a flash. Mme Sandrine Albright, who signs herself Sandrine, Domaine Verdier. Albright, it is not a very French name, there is a story here that might explain her good grasp of English. Seeing as she has just taken a seat between me and Emil, the man from Common Market, I might get a chance to ask.

Emil and Sandrine are quickly into a discussion about the future of wine production. The reform Emil saw as needed, to get away from high volume, low-quality and high-subsidy production before the Common Market drowns in a sea of plonk. Sandrine's ambition to make wines that were good enough to compete for a place on the Wine List of quality restaurants alongside the wines of Bordeaux and Burgundy.

It is an interesting conversation but more interesting to me is the young, fresh, rosé wine we are drinking with the *Salade de Gesiers* entrée. It almost sparkles on my palette; I taste strawberries and rose petals on every mouthful.

"Cinsault, one hundred per cent." I catch the key words as I come out with my English language reverie.

"A nice wine, last year's?" I am genuinely interested. Currently, the market for rosé in Britain is limited. Mostly you get Mateus Rosé from Portugal and a little sweet Anjou rosé from the Loire. This is a drier wine than either, not that I would say it nowadays, less feminine. I might be able to do something with this.

"Oui, we made four hundred bottles, this is almost the last. Mind you, the vines are looking better this year and with the extra planting we hope for a three-fold increase in the grapes harvested this year."

Mme Verdier, Hélène, clears the table and Sandrine excuses herself to help her mother. I turn to Emil. "What do you think of this?" I held up my glass of bright, pink wine to the sun to remind myself of the clarity and intensity of the colour.

Emil swirled the wine in his glass, stuck his nose into the glass and inhaled. "It is not exceptional, but it is a wine of great quality. If Mme Sandrine continues to develop it, it would grace any table."

I couldn't help but agree with him.

The aroma that escapes from the casserole pot when the lid is removed is to die for. *Confit de Canard,* a cooked and preserved duck, slowly cooked in a sauce of fresh cherries, to accompany it, a bowl of green beans topped with a rapidly melting mountain of pale-yellow butter and a red wine. A red wine light on tannins and rich on black and red fruits, a wine with enough 'oomph', a technical term for, well, 'oomph!' I can't think of another word for it. Enough oomph to carry through the rich sauce and fattiness of the duck, without overpowering either. A wine that had longevity on the tongue that did not clog the taste buds. I was sold.

"What do you think, M Thornton?"

"Charles, please M. Verdier. I was just about to ask Sandrine how many bottles of this wine she has available."

"Sandrine, did you catch that?"

"Yes, Papa I heard. We have enough to meet your order, Charles. What do you think of that Emil?" A quality wine from La Domaine Verdier being sold to the English!

"I am not surprised. It is a good wine. It compares well with the stuff we used to send to Germany as vintage Bordeaux in the forties."

That stops me dead in my tracks. It seems to surprise Sandrine too. On the other hand, M. Verdier seems totally unperturbed.

"I see I need to explain that statement." Emil began to explain his role in Bordeaux, working as a translator for the German Wehrmacht in the office of the Weinführer. During that time, he had been drawn into the world of wine. He described with laughter how, if the Weinführer disliked the official placing an order, they would receive 'special' bottlings, bottles filled with the requested vintage … blended with a significant and varying percentage of wine from the Languedoc. The exact percentage of each wine depending on how much he disliked the man it was going to.

Sandrine seemed to be emboldened by this story. "So, there is a history of wines from this region being served at the dining tables of the powerful men!"

"It has been like that ever since at least the start of the century, if the rumours I have heard are true," I point out. It is a badly kept secret, people in the trade occasionally picked up a change in the taste between the tasting in Bordeaux and after shipping to Britain, the wines didn't travel well.

France 1974 – Dessert

The apricot tarte tatin, which was served with a sweetened *Schlagsahne* cream, was light and simple. I must admit I am surprised that the Englishman, Charles Thornton, is so sanguine about the adulterating story. I thought it was a well-kept secret. He just carried on as if it was an everyday conversation. Then he turns to Papa Verdier.

"M. Verdier," for an Englishman his French is quite good, "I see you know all about the blending that goes on in some Bordeaux Houses."

The Frenchman nodded, and his daughter exclaimed "Papa! You knew about this?"

"I knew, I know about it." He confirmed.

"You know about it?" Sandrine must have notice the use of the present tense too. "It is still happening?"

"Where do you think the extra money for the cars and tractors comes from? Why our Co-operative buys at such a high price? I have no proof of where the extra money comes from, beyond the tankers with Bordeaux addresses that collect twice a week." He turns to me, adding, "I declare the real price we get on our forms."

"M. Verdier, today I am on holiday, tasting wonderful food and excellent wines," I raise my glass to salute the two ladies responsible. "I am enjoying a conversation about the future of wine from this region with a purchaser, a producer and her mentor, on a summer afternoon. Let us drink to good food, good company and honest conversation!"

"Food, company and conversation!" Charles raises his glass. "What say you, M. Verdier?"

"In that case, I am Louis! To friendships!"

He had hardly raised his glass, when the Englishman started to choke on his wine. His charming wife mopped him down with a napkin, while he tried to regain his composure. Eventually, the wild look in his eyes calmed and his breathing returned to near normal. We settled back down again. Then Charles asked an unexpected question.

"M. Verdier, Louis, how did you come to injure your arm?" I had hardly noticed but yes, the farmer held his left arm stiffly.

"It was in the war; a bomb fell on it!" He made it sound like a joke, except it wasn't. I suddenly realised that it was I, as in me, from my personal knowledge knew that it wasn't a joke. To Helga and the others, it might still be a humorous deflection. I let the conversation between Charles and Louis continue as the images from years before flashed before my eyes.

"Trapping you under a damaged aircraft?" How did Charles know? This was getting weird.

"Yes, then there was an attack by some German aircraft, killing a lot of my comrades-in-arms, the rest ran away." Silence had fallen around the table, I'm not sure this story had ever been told quite like this before. "The bomb was dislodged trapping me. Then an English pilot appeared and tried to help. Before he could do much the Boches, sorry, Germans, arrived. Between them, the Englishman and a German who spoke good French … they got me out." Louis' eyes fixed on me as he finished the sentence.

"Then the bloody Luftwaffe turned up and bombed us all again!" Who said that? Was that me? Was it Louis? Or was that the Englishman speaking? How could he know?

Edward Yeoman

France 1994

That had been the minute my Papa's life changed. The two men who had hidden under the wing of a wrecked plane with my injured father all those years ago had been guided back to our farm, by separate paths but in an act of synchronicity. I am not sure which of the many gods, wine, war or even love had brought them to our table that day, but it was the start of something wonderful.

It was the start of a friendship between the three families that will last beyond today.

That afternoon, they had each gone over every detail of the incident they could remember. It fitted together perfectly. Thirty-four years after they had met, three frightened young men, who chose not to kill each other were reunited.

I suppose I shouldn't have been surprised by the fact that their wives had struck up an instant rapport. All were almost exactly the same age. They had two children each. They had lived through the hardship, deprivation and the pain of loss that war had brought them. Then they all had that thing with the 'H' names that had been the first thing they shared together.

Over the years since then, we have

shared many happy times together. Their grandchildren, our children and our children's children have exchanged homes for holidays and language lessons. We have become something truly European; it would be as impossible for them to kill another just because of their nationality. Maybe this time it really was the war that ended war in Europe.

Then over the past few years, they have slipped away, the elders at that table on that June day. Emil taken with a cancer. Heather going into hospital for a routine operation and never coming out. Helga falling asleep. Mama, sitting by the fire on a winter's afternoon. Charles, who had stood next to my Papa at Mama's funeral, supporting him to the very last, had succumbed to a second stroke just a few weeks later. Now Papa.

He had failed to appear for lunch, we found him an hour or so later. He had ridden the heavily modified golf-cart he called his Quadbike up the hill to the stand of ancient olives that are hidden from the house but overlook the village of Perinac. He was lying, looking like he was just dozing on the grass, one arm out as if embracing someone. It was the spot he claimed he and Mama used to hide from her husband, Henri, and where they created me.

Now I am standing at the side of his grave, in our little farm graveyard. His is the second grave on 'our' side of the walled enclosure next to Mama. On the opposite side, the Menton line ends in a simple stone commemorating Henri Menton.

Michael, my second husband, has shepherded the children and grandchildren, the friends and colleagues away to the house to leave us a few minutes to say farewell to a generation. I raise my head and my eyes met my brother, Henri's. It is time to re-join the living. Gilles takes one of my arms and Dieter the other, while Sophie and Antja take up position alongside Henri. We walk back to the house to be part of the wake at the house.

Tomorrow is Henri's birthday, and according to family tradition the sixtieth anniversary of my conception. The family will celebrate with a party underneath the walnut trees.

Thinking about it as we walk towards tomorrow, I come to the conclusion that it was the god, Hermes, who was the key player in this story. After all, he is the ancient Greek god of trade, wealth, luck, fertility, language and travel. One of the cleverest and most mischievous of the Olympian gods.

Thank you for the lives of Charles and Emil, through them you gave me a father's love. Thank you, Hermes.

Edward Yeoman

Tomorrow is …

The Last Day of June 1994

ABOUT THE AUTHOR

Ted Bun was born in South London too many years ago. He was educated at Gillingham Grammar and the University of Kent. Where he obtained a very useful degree in Microbiology. After spending years pursuing what is now called a 'portfolio career;' he retired. He now lives in a small house in the South of France with his wife Valerie. It is here he discovered what he really wanted to do in life and writes.

Printed in Great Britain
by Amazon

42513666R00111